It had sounded like such a good idea.

A run with five thousand people dressed as Santa. That way, her family wouldn't get noticed and maybe burn off the animosity that had formed between them.

She had found the run and went to her father, Santa Claus, for permission. His eyes had lit up at the very thought. *A competition! That's perfect.*

He had given a week in the middle of the busiest time of the year to go to Las Vegas and maybe hash out the differences.

Her siblings had agreed to several rules to participate in the run and the first one was no magic.

Which was turning out to be a disaster.

Praise for Kristine Grayson

"With her series of magical romances, Kristine Grayson has carved out her own special and unique place in the romance genre."

— RT BOOK REVIEWS

"The reigning queen of paranormal romance."

— THE BEST REVIEWS

"...[Kristine Grayson] will have a long and glorious career."

— THE ROMANCE READER.COM

"Kristine Grayson gives 'happily ever after' her own unique twist!"

— KASEY MICHAELS

"Grayson's clever, humor-tinged writing is absolutely delightful."

— BOOKLIST

The Santa Series

READING ORDER

THE SANTA SERIES

Up on the Rooftop

Visions of Sugar Plums

Dressed in Holiday Style

Tidings of Comfort and Joy

Santa Claus Lane

All the books in The Santa Series *standalone and can be read out of order. However, some books have characters from the previous stories in them.*

THE FATES UNIVERSE

THE FATES TRILOGY

Simply Irresistible

Absolutely Captivated

Totally Spellbound

THE DAUGHTERS OF ZEUS TRILOGY

Tiffany Tumbles

Crystal Caves

Brittany Bends

OTHER BOOKS IN THE FATES UNIVERSE

Completely Smitten

The Charming Trilogy, Vol. 1

The Charming Trilogy, Vol. 2

Also by Kristine Grayson (Writing as Kristine Kathryn Rusch)

WORLD OF THE FEY

THE ORIGINAL BOOKS OF THE FEY

The Sacrifice: Book One of the Fey

The Changeling: Book Two of the Fey

The Rival: Book Three of the Fey

The Resistance: Book Four of the Fey

Victory: Book Five of the Fey

THE BLACK THRONE

The Black Queen: Book One of the Black Throne

The Black King: Book Two of the Black Throne

Searching for the Fleet: A Diving Novel

The Spires of Denon: A Diving Universe Novella

The Renegat: A Diving Universe Novel

Escaping Amnthra: A Diving Universe Novella

The Court-Martial of the Renegat Renegades

Thieves: A Diving Novel

Squishy's Teams: A Diving Universe Novel

The Chase: A Diving Novel

Maelstrom: A Diving Universe Novella

THE RETRIEVAL ARTIST SERIES

The Disappeared

Extremes

Consequences

Buried Deep

Paloma

Recovery Man

The Recovery Man's Bargain

Duplicate Effort

The Possession of Paavo Deshin

Anniversary Day

Blowback

A Murder of Clones

Search & Recovery

The Peyti Crisis

Vigilantes

Starbase Human

Masterminds

The Impossibles

The Retrieval Artist

Writing as Kris Nelscott

THE SMOKEY DALTON SERIES

A Dangerous Road

Smoke-Filled Rooms

Thin Walls

Stone Cribs

War at Home

Days of Rage

Street Justice

Santa Claus Lane

THE SANTA SERIES

KRISTINE GRAYSON

WMG
PUBLISHING

Santa Claus Lane

Copyright © 2012 by Kristine Grayson

Published by WMG Publishing

Interior design by Stephanie Writt | WMG Publishing

Cover design © 2024 Kim Killion Group

Book & Pen Art © Canva

ISBN-13 (trade paperback): 978-1-56146-125-7

ISBN-13 (hardcover): 978-1-56146-133-2

Santa Claus Lane

"This is stupid," Tahvo said, clutching the cheap plastic bag to his chest. "We shouldn't even be here."

He glared at Pippa, then let the line of mortals see his distress. The line extended around the entire back side of the thrift store, heading toward the doors to the warehouse.

Despite the grayish-white fluorescent lighting, Tahvo still looked tanned and handsome, his white-blond hair glinting as if the lighting was just made for him. But his bright-blue eyes weren't sparkling, and his bow-shaped mouth was turned down.

A furious S-Elf was as formidable as a charming one. Pippa had known that but had forgotten it. She hadn't had to face her family's wrath over anything in a very long time.

Tahvo gave her one more hard look, then threaded his way through a tight aisle of used clothing and then past tables covered in old shoes. Pippa should have hurried to keep up with him, stop him, and then cajole him to return to the line, but she didn't. She felt humiliated enough.

She looked at the bags piled on the sign-up tables by size. She hadn't realized that the Santa costumes would be so cheap, like some kind of poorly made knockoff. The sizing didn't make sense to anyone except the volunteers in the back of the thrift store warehouse, where dozens of regular people were lined up to get their costumes.

Her siblings—S-Elves all—had clustered around her. Someone—maybe her brother Niko—had suggested that only one of them come to pick up the packets, but she hadn't listened to him.

No one listened to Niko anymore since he had taken himself out of the running for the Big Job. Not that they had listened to him before. He had only come to this gathering because she had begged him.

She had resolved, as she stood in that line, that she would listen to him for the rest of the week. Of all Santa's six children, Niko was the only one who lived in the Greater World and had done so for a long time. He knew how it all worked.

Now she had to calm down her family, and that was always difficult.

Her sister Saara followed Tahvo out of the thrift store as if his irritation was hers as well. Three of her other siblings had just received their packets as Tahvo passed them, making his snide remarks. She had opted to go last so that she could make sure everyone had picked up the things they needed for the charity race on Saturday.

It had sounded like such a good idea. A run with five thousand people dressed as Santa. That way, her family wouldn't get noticed, and maybe, just maybe, something like a race would burn off the animosity that had formed between all of them.

Back in July, she had gone to see the Big Guy, which was what everyone called their dad—even the North siblings—and told him he needed to step in. His children were constantly fighting, and that wasn't a good look for Santa's family.

He had waved a pudgy hand in dismissal. He had just returned from his second—and last—journey of the year to Hawaii and was getting ready for the final sprint to the Big Day. She had thought it would be a good time to talk with him. He was tanned, rested, and ready to work.

Instead, he had given her an odd look.

Check out the family history, young'un, he said, using the nickname for her that she hated more than Pipsqueak. *The S-Elves of the Santa line always fight with each other. That's how we determine who is the strongest for the job.*

She hated that. She was tired of fighting with her siblings. She wasn't even sure she wanted to be Santa

Claus. Part of her envied Niko, who had taken himself out of the running years ago.

Maybe that was why she suggested a Santa run. Maybe she wanted to be as far from the North Pole in the holiday season as possible.

She had found the run and went to her father for permission. After all, every one of his children would be gone for a long weekend in the month before the Big Day.

But his eyes had lit up at the very thought. *A competition! That's perfect. I knew you would come around, Pippa.*

She hadn't thought of it that way. She had just figured it would burn off some of the negative energy around all of them and then maybe give them a chance to talk.

At one point, she had considered canceling the entire thing, but her father had fallen in love with it. He had given those who wanted the time a week in the middle of the busiest time of the year to go to Las Vegas, camp out in three gigantic adjacent suites she had rented in the city's newest hotel, and maybe hash out the differences.

And on top of all that, everything would end with a silly run that wasn't even timed, although the Norths had all agreed to wear a timing chip on their bibs—chips that Pippa had bought herself.

They had to agree to several rules to participate in the run itself, and the first one—the main one—was no magic. They couldn't beat the mortal Santas by using powers that no mortal had.

If they were going to run in the mortal world, then

they were going to run. And they were going to follow all the rules of the race, including the in-person packet pickup.

Which was turning out to be a disaster.

The women behind the table were very cheerful. The mortals in line were also cheerful. Pippa's family was *not* cheerful, grimacing as they got the packet she had paid for.

But only Tahvo had been ungracious enough to comment on the cheap quality of the Santa suit inside the packet—and fortunately, he had done so as he passed Pippa, adding his *stupid* comment as he went by.

Her cheeks heated so badly that she probably matched the suit. The woman behind the table, who took her name —all of the Norths, in fact—had given Pippa an empathetic look.

It was embarrassing in the extreme, especially since S-Elves had so much charm that no one should have registered any disagreement among them as a disagreement. It should have seemed, to the average mortal, like some kind of charming discourse filled with just a touch of joy.

That was what S-Elves specialized in, supposedly. Everyone in Santa's line had the ability to make any mortal (anyone, really) around them feel better for the encounter.

"Sorry," Pippa said as she reached the front of the line. "My brother's a little stressed this time of year. He's working too hard."

"I understand, honey," the woman said as she grabbed

a paper bib, a plastic bag with a red suit inside, and some flyers and stuffed them into a used plastic bag. "The race will soften him. You'll see."

"I hope so," Pippa said and didn't add *because right now, this is looking like a disaster.*

THE
Santa
SERIES

Two

Anton Walker watched a tall, blond guy stomp away from the sign-up tables. He didn't quite push past the line of people waiting patiently for their suits, but he didn't try hard to avoid them either.

Who does that, anyway? People were here to have a good time. The blond jerk and his matching blond—wife? Sister?—hurried away from the table as if the items on it were going to bite them.

Anton put his hand on his daughter Lila's head. Her coiled brown curls were pressed tightly against his palm. He hoped she hadn't seen the interaction. It had been hard enough to get her to come here.

She was clinging to his waist, her head buried in his crisp white shirt like she had done a few months ago when he had signed her up for school here in Las Vegas. She would have had a tough time with the transfer normally—any kid would—but she was doing it in a new city in the middle of the semester. Add losing her mom on top of it, and Lila was having just about the worst year anyone could have.

He glanced down at her, and to his dismay, she was watching those entitled-looking blonds get their packets. It was clear they were all related—a good-looking family, if you liked clichéd Northern European types.

The blond guy who had spoken—and who was now halfway down the aisle of repurposed clothes—had a bit of an accent, too, one Anton couldn't place.

The four others who remained closely resembled each other. There was an apple-cheeked woman with tight blond braids who looked like she had stepped out of an ancient version of *Heidi*. Her bright red mouth was in a moue of distaste, which seemed very similar to the look that the tall blond guy had when he broke open the edge of his packet and fingered the suit inside.

"We're expected to wear this?" he had asked the volunteer behind the table.

"No, sir," she had said diplomatically. "You may wear whatever you want."

After hearing that, he had immediately pivoted and glared at the last blond in line, a young athletic woman whose face Anton couldn't quite see but who seemed to have the exact same body structure as the others.

They moved alike and seemed related, but he couldn't

quite figure out the relationships. Body language told him that two of the women and at least one of the men—the jerk who stalked off—didn't want to be there at all.

Anton had no idea why people had to share their bad moods with everyone else. Nor did he understand why people were in a bad mood here. He had participated in the Run On Santa Claus Lane in Las Vegas years ago when he was still playing basketball professionally. Someone had figured out that he lived in Las Vegas and convinced him to act as grand marshal.

He had flown in from Dallas after a hard-fought game, irritated that he had agreed to participate when he only had two days between games and left thinking that the joy he had seen was something that had been missing from his life.

He'd used that moment as a mental touchstone for years, reminding himself that he *played* a game. Yes, it was work, but it was also *play*. And there should be joy in play.

Lila's arm tightened around his waist as the line moved ever so slightly forward. He moved his hand to her shoulder, squeezing it in what he hoped was reassurance.

He had brought her here in the hopes that this event would bring a little joy into her life as it had to his all those years ago, even though her therapist had told him not to push her grieving process.

She's lost everything, the therapist had said, and then she had flushed a little to quickly correct herself. *Except you.*

But the therapist had been right the first time. Anton hadn't been raising Lila. He'd only had her during summers when he was still playing professional basketball. She would arrive in mid-June (so that he could account for the hope that his team would make the playoffs) and leave before Labor Day.

After that, he would tell her mother he was simply too busy to take her as if she were a burden rather than a child. He just figured her mom could handle her. After all, Cherise had gotten pregnant deliberately, trying to force him to marry her. That hadn't worked. He supported his daughter from the time she was in the womb, but he wasn't going to be forced to marry a woman that it turned out he didn't even like.

To be fair, though, Cherise had been a good mother. She had dropped her basketball groupie behavior, gotten a good job, and used his money properly to take care of their daughter. They'd lived in a house he bought in Brentwood before he'd been traded out of LA, and Cherise had built their life there.

A life a drunk driver had ruined one late September night, leaving Lila—and, truth be told, Anton—reeling.

"I want to go home," Lila said quietly. Everything she said was quiet now. But at least she was calling his sprawling house in Summerlin home now. That was, as the therapist told him, a step forward.

Baby steps, the therapist had said. *You'll watch her get through this one tiny step at a time.*

"We will leave soon," he said. "We just need to get the packets."

He had hoped to take her to her favorite diner after they picked up the packets. He wanted to treat her to a milkshake just for coming out with him.

And maybe he would. He would see if he could convince her.

"Those white people are rude," Lila said, maybe a tad too loudly. She was watching the blonds, then, too.

"I think the rude ones just left." He nodded toward the remaining blonde, who was standing in front of the volunteer who took the brunt of the jerk's anger. "See? I think that woman's apologizing."

"Someone should," Lila said. "Because this is supposed to be fun."

He smiled down at her. *Home* and *fun* in the same conversation. A little progress, anyway.

"We'll have fun," he said.

"Not with people like that, we won't," Lila said.

It always amazed him how observant she was and how big her vocabulary was. Some of that was due to the hugely expensive private schools that Cherise had put her in from the time she could walk, but some of that was pure Lila.

She was smarter than any kid—any person—he'd ever met. That one fact had sent him scrambling the week of Cherise's death. He'd finally had to call the retired player's association and ask for help finding her a similar school here in Las Vegas. And, if truth be told, ensuring that she would get in.

Everyone kept saying he should move to Los Angeles and let Lila continue in her same school, live in the same neighborhood (same house, even), and move on slowly with her life.

But his life was here, in Vegas. He worked with the association now, helping retired basketball players negotiate the financial problems that came with being a young man in a sport that paid them boatloads of money...until, maybe suddenly, it didn't.

So he moved her, and that was when she got really quiet. Not the rambunctious child he'd always worked to corral.

She had gotten his height and her mother's beauty. And those smarts. He hadn't pushed Lila to try sports at all. This run would be the first thing that they were doing that would be anything remotely like a sport, and they were walking the mile, which would be hard enough on him. He was on his fifth surgery for the destroyed knee that had abruptly ended his career. Or rather, he was going to have his fifth surgery as soon as Lila got settled. But he had no idea how long that would take.

Nor did he know how long it would take him to get used to her. He was trying to do all the care, even though he had a housekeeper. He hadn't hired a nanny, despite what his friends told him to do.

Cherise hadn't had a nanny either, even though he'd

offered to pay for one. He could still hear the contempt in her voice: *Farm out raising my baby to someone I pay? I got this, Anton. She's gonna have* our *values, not the values of someone whose family we don't know.*

He had never explained to Cherise's mother that he knew his own family's values and that he wasn't going to raise Lila like that. He hadn't even asked his mother to come help in those early weeks, even though Cherise's mother had been in and out.

He'd encouraged her to spend time with her remaining children this December. And she had teared up, maybe at the word "remaining." Saying that was one of those things he couldn't take back.

But she had taken his advice, promising she would return off and on during the season. Despite their past, he actually looked forward to her visiting. Once Cherise's mother had gotten past her anger at him for refusing to marry her baby, she had formed a friendship with him, one Cherise wasn't sure she liked.

Not that it mattered now.

Except to Lila.

"I don't like white people," Lila said.

She'd said that before, and it bothered him. Half the people he worked with were white. Many of his friends were white.

Cherise hadn't taught her that. Cherise's mother had been appalled the first time she heard Lila say it.

The therapist finally figured out what was going on.

The drunk driver, the therapist had said. *He was white.*

Yeah, Anton had said.

And she hears the news because you keep it on all the time. Right now, there's a divide. Listen to the news on your own time, Anton.

So he had. But he also worried about her, like any Black father would about raising their child in this hideously polarized world. He had planned to work with the therapist after the new year about figuring out how to protect his daughter without her internalizing all of the bad stuff.

Until then, he was going to have to deal with it as best as he could.

"There are rude people of every skin color, Lila," he said softly.

"I guess," Lila said, sounding unconvinced. "But those people are just mean."

THE
Santa
SERIES

Three

Pippa scurried down the aisles of the thrift store, face warm and feeling like everyone in the place was watching her. Even though the volunteer had been friendly and understanding, some of the people in line had been glaring at Pippa as if that little interaction had been all her fault.

In truth, it had been. She should have known better. Nothing she planned with her siblings ever worked out.

Pippa was the youngest by quite a bit. Niko was the closest to her in age, and he was eight years older than she was. Pippa had been—in her mother's words—a delightful surprise. Maybe Pippa had been delightful to her parents, but she had been either a stunning ray of momentary cuteness to her siblings or an underfoot nuisance.

More often than not, she had been the nuisance, at least if their behavior had been any indication.

The fact that they had allowed her to plan this trip spoke of their desperation to resolve the inheritance controversy once and for all.

She was the last person out of the thrift store. It was in a neighborhood far from the Strip, filled with sun-bleached buildings that had seen better days. There was a new gas station across the street and a chain restaurant, but everything else looked like it had been here for decades.

The entire neighborhood made her feel deflated. The pictures she had seen of the Run On Santa Claus Lane, which benefited this charity, had looked like fun, but the thrift store and the cheap costumes didn't give her a lot of hope.

She opened the sliding door to the van she had rented and climbed in. The back seated six, but only four of her siblings sat there. Arja, the oldest, sat up front in the passenger seat as if she knew everywhere anyone was going.

She wore her blond hair in a long single braid that at the moment, she had wrapped around the top of her head. It made her look like a clichéd member of the von Trapp family. She wore a red-and-green sweater with embroidered reindeer on it and an appliqué skirt that went past her knees.

She was clearly doing everything she could to look as

out of place as possible. Since she arrived the day before, she hadn't said more than five sentences to Pippa, and one of those sentences had been just *Hello*.

Niko was driving. When Pippa planned the trip, he had volunteered. He had taken driving lessons when he moved to the Greater World permanently and claimed he liked to drive. Pippa had checked with his wife, Raine, to make sure that he could drive well enough to ferry them all over Las Vegas, and Raine had confirmed it.

Pippa met Raine six months before at a wedding. It was the first time anyone from the North Pole had met Niko's family, which already included a daughter who had charmed everyone (showing her heritage) and a newborn son whose cheeks were candy-apple red from birth.

It had been Raine's idea to have Niko come without her and the children. She had said to Pippa, *He wants to be a part of the family again, but he isn't sure anyone wants him.*

Well, Pippa wanted him. It had felt like she had lost a limb when Niko turned his back on the North Pole. They hadn't been very close, but they had been close enough that Pippa had relied on him to talk her down when she got upset, to put the family into perspective, or to help her with a myriad of small things that were unique to the North family of the North Pole.

Like Arja, he hadn't said much to her either. He had arrived late the night before, taking an actual flight from Chicago. He was the only one who had used a commercial airline instead of just magically appearing at an agreed spot near the hotel.

Apparently, he used mortal transportation a lot because he had an actual business here, which was one of the biggest charities in the state of Illinois. He hoped to expand it and to do that, he had become a regular flier, mostly because his contacts expected to meet him at the airport.

He had been quiet all day. With Tahvo's help, Niko was able to use the GPS in the van to get them wherever they needed to go.

Niko looked very serious but softer somehow. All the North siblings had wheat-blond hair and an angular bone structure that vanished as they put on weight. They had blue eyes so stunning that any one of the siblings who spent a lot of time in the mortal world usually wore sunglasses so no one could see just how bright their eyes were.

Their skin was white as snow. Their mother used to describe them all with a laugh since she was not as depicted in the literature. She was native Hawaiian, which gave her the figure of the woman in all of the drawings but not the coloring. No one in their family had gotten her coloring, and she blamed that on the S-Elf magic. She was probably right.

All of the North siblings had the power to make people's wishes come true—as long as those wishes were an actual something and as long as they were truly a wish and not a want. It was a power that could not be used lightly or for any fraudulent purpose.

It was a violation for an S-Elf to make someone act against their conscience or their own desires, and those violations could mount up and lead to a removal of powers. Apparently that had happened to their father's great-granduncle, whom some said became the model for Krampus, although Pippa had never seen any evidence to support that theory.

She had tried to ask their father about it, but he had said that he did not like to dwell on the dark side of family history and refused to talk about it anymore.

"Hotel?" Niko asked.

"Yeah," Tahvo said, even though he had promised he wouldn't try to take over everything. "We gotta look at these lovely outfits that Pippa wants us to wear."

"Tahv," Saara said with a disapproving tone that only she could manage. "Settle down."

Saara was the one whom their father called "the peacemaker," although sometimes Pippa thought she used her status as the second born to stir things up just so she could settle them down.

There was no one in the family that Pippa fought with more than Saara, who just didn't seem to like her very much. Pippa supposed that was normal in any large family, but it still made her uncomfortable.

And it shouldn't have. Saara, after all, was the only one who thanked her for signing them up for this race, which surprised Pippa. Saara rarely complimented her on anything.

Then Saara explained why she was saying thank you, and of course, it hadn't been about the family. It had been about Saara.

I decided to train, Saara had told her the week before they left, *and I've lost thirty pounds*.

Because she had, her angular bone structure was visible once again. She wore leggings now and running shoes and hoodies with slogans. Today's was simple and obvious: *Christmas comes but once a year*.

Just like everything else, Pippa had wanted to say when she had seen the slogan, but she hadn't because she had learned to hold her tongue around Saara.

"What, Saara, I can't note my dissatisfaction?" Tahvo said. "This is the *worst* time of year for me to be here. You know that."

Niko's shoulders went up and down in a silent sigh. He moved some lever on the steering wheel and pulled the van around the parking lot.

"It's a bad time for all of us," Joulu said from beside Pippa. He didn't look at her. He, at least, did not look like a North Pole refugee, which was probably deliberate since his name was Norwegian and sounded very similar to "yule." He was wearing a thin blue hoodie with a Nike logo and blue jeans. His hair was neatly trimmed against his scalp, and in his right hand, he held his sunglasses, which had round bright-blue lenses.

He hadn't said anything to anyone, but unless Pippa missed her guess, he had come to the Greater World a lot more often than he had let on.

"The Big Guy approved it," Pippa said, hating that she sounded so defensive.

"He didn't just approve it," Saara said in that sickly sweet voice she used when she had a secret that no one else did.

Pippa tensed, waiting for the knife to stick in because that was how Saara used that voice—as a blade.

"He called us and reminded us that we were obligated to come."

Pippa flushed again, and this time, she closed her eyes, feeling the tears well and hoping she could stave them off. She hadn't realized their father was forcing everyone to come. She had thought—

Well, she had thought that maybe they really wanted to work out their differences and end the rivalry once and for all.

"Nice to see that the viciousness of the current North clan is alive and well," Niko said just loud enough for everyone to hear.

Pippa opened her eyes. Her gaze met his in the rearview mirror, and unless she missed her guess, he was looking at her with something akin to compassion.

She gave him a tiny smile and looked down, wishing that she had more control over her emotions. The fact that their father was forcing everyone to come

—that hurt. It hurt more than she wanted to knowledge.

"What do you care?" Arja said in a low voice as if the people in the back couldn't hear what the people in the front were discussing. "You've abandoned the family entirely."

Niko grunted ever so softly. "If you look at the history, Arja, the family abandoned me long before I ever walked away."

"Stop," Tahvo said. "I didn't mean to start the bickering. It's just—security has gotten weird during the internet age, and the threats to our private little compound have gotten worse over the past decade or so. I have a good team, but sometimes that's not enough."

He tried to sound calm, but he didn't. Pippa turned so she could see him in the seat behind them.

"I didn't know," she said.

"No one does, not really," Tahvo said. "I try not to burden the Big Guy with it all, but we're going to need more magic on the perimeter. Internet sleuths are working very hard to find us, podcasters who believe they know the secret to the North Pole, and a handful of people with their own levels of magic who can get through the holes in our protective bubble."

"You should stop worrying," Joulu said. "You have a good team."

"I do, but we're understaffed." Tahvo had set his suit on the seat beside him, but his hand still rested on the plastic wrapping, crinkling it. The sound was as irritating as fingers on a blackboard, but Pippa didn't say anything.

This was the first time Tahvo had ever spoken of anything like this—at least in her presence.

"All it takes is one these days," Tahvo said. "One person to break through, and then we'll get hordes. Because one will break through and post what they've done, and other people will try it, and we won't be able to keep up."

"We've kept up in the past," Saara said as if she was trying to be soothing. She wasn't. She was rebuking him.

"In the past, people didn't use technology. Not everyone in the North Pole can fight a technological battle," Tahvo said. "Most of us can't reliably use a cell phone."

And then he looked pointedly at Niko, who had figured out how to drive and not cause issues on planes or public transportation but couldn't make GPS work at all. Niko had a cell phone because his wife Raine insisted on it, but he couldn't carry it on his person the entire time he was gone, or the cell phone would die. They had worked something out—what, Pippa didn't know—and it seemed to work for them.

She'd only seen Niko and Raine together once, and that was more than enough to make Pippa envious of him. He had found someone who not only loved him but understood him. Pippa hadn't even thought that was possible.

Her parents loved each other but operated on a very old-fashioned model. Her mother supported her father 100 percent and had literally given up everything in her previous life to become his wife. She fit into the mold as best she could—round, jolly, nurturing—even though she had been extremely controversial in her day because she hadn't looked the role, at least what the Old Men in Charge thought the role should look like.

And now, there were three S-Elves—Santa's daughters—who might succeed him. There was already a lot of discussion about what might happen if they became Santa. Would they have to look like their father did? Would they need to have the long white beard and emit deep masculine chuckles? Or would they be able to remake the role anew?

Arja was aching to find out. She wanted that opportunity more than any of them—at least as far as Pippa was concerned. Saara had been researching previous Santas. She was of the belief that Santa had been female more than once, but had always conformed.

There was no doubt that was what she would do as well.

And Pippa? Pippa wasn't sure what she wanted. She knew what was expected of her, but she was very intrigued by her brother Niko, who seemed to have remade his family heritage in a positive way in the Greater World. She hoped to get a chance to talk with him about it at some point.

Right now, though, he was driving them cautiously through streets filled with ranch houses and Christmas lights against a desert landscape.

"You're here," Niko said without looking at any of them. Maybe he wasn't just talking to Tahvo. Maybe he was talking to everyone. "You might as well enjoy it."

"I don't run," Arja said for maybe the eightieth time.

"I wouldn't worry about it," Joulu said. "It's not as if the winner of the family race is going to get the nod to become Santa."

"Then why do we have timing chips?" Arja asked. She half turned around in her seat so she could look at Pippa.

There's no guarantee they'll work given who we are, Pippa almost said but stopped herself. She wasn't going to be defensive about this.

"I figured the timing chips would make this more interesting," she said, which was also true.

Arja sighed. "I don't want to wear it," she said.

"Just go out there and enjoy yourself," Niko said with more annoyance than Pippa expected. "We all came—"

"Some of us under duress," Tahvo said.

"—and we haven't ever been alone like this before, not as adults." Niko used one hand to turn the steering wheel down a very busy six-lane street. He didn't seem worried about all the traffic, but it sure put Pippa on edge.

Maybe she should have hired a real driver after all. At least a local would have known the best routes, maybe the ones that avoided lots and lots and lots of cars.

"So?" Arja said, with a bit of an edge in her voice.

"So maybe we should get to know one another as adults," Niko said.

Pippa held her breath. She had hoped for that, too, but she hadn't said it. Saying it would have been too much of a risk.

"Why?" Arja asked. "Just because we're related?"

Niko let out a small breath and shook his head. "Not all of us are being competitive over the Big Guy's job."

"Yes," Arja said. "Some of us figured we weren't suited for it and bowed out early. I should thank you for that."

Niko's cheeks flushed. His hand tightened on the steering wheel. That was the kind of rejection that he had clearly feared coming here, and Pippa had just let it happen.

"Was there any reason to be mean?" Pippa asked before she could stop the words from coming out of her mouth.

"It wasn't mean," Arja said. "It was true."

"The truth can be mean," Joulu muttered.

Pippa hated how this was going. "Niko is really suited for the job, maybe more than all the rest of us combined. You should see what he's doing in Chicago. He's helping more people there than we help these days. He's figured out how to help children that we can't even—"

"Don't, Pippa," Niko said. "It doesn't matter. Arja's right. I am not suited for the job as it is now. Maybe I never was."

The key phrase was *as it is now*. Pippa understood what he meant. She remembered his fights with the Old Men in Charge, as well as the Big Guy, trying to get them to change policies and procedures that had been instituted more than a century ago.

Pippa flounced backward, arms crossed. She wasn't sure now what she had wanted from this trip, but she knew it wasn't this.

Maybe she should call it all off. But now, with their father involved, that might not be an option.

And what did he want anyway? His kids to get along? Or an end to the competition? Did he somehow see the race as a definitive point in the battle to become the next Santa?

She didn't know, and she didn't want to ask him. She felt betrayed by him. If he had wanted everyone to come, shouldn't he have told her?

Her father was not the kind of man who tried to support Pippa in her goals and dreams. He was, at best, a distant father who had more important things to do than to pay attention to his children, particularly when they were little.

And yes, she understood the irony of that. He took care of the world's children, but he couldn't be bothered with his own. That was for their mother. She took care of home and hearth while he built toys for all.

Or something like that.

Pippa blinked hard, hating that the tears still threatened. Even when she tried to avoid him, her father still influenced everything.

"You know," she said after a moment. "You can all go home if you want. I'm not going to fight any of you over this. Just go. You all have more important things to do."

Her words were greeted with silence. And then Tahvo said, "I actually do."

He tossed his plastic package on the seat beside her, put his right forefinger on the side of his nose, and nodded his head. Then he vanished, leaving the air where he had been filled with little snowflake-like sparkles.

Pippa felt her heart sink. She hated that. She could do it, too, but she didn't. She thought just disappearing on people was rude.

"I agree with Tahvo," Arja said. "There are more important things in this world than your little run."

And she used the same trick—finger beside the nose, a nod, and all that remained were sparkles.

Niko drove the van over a little rise between intersections, heading toward the Strip and the gigantic hotel tower where Pippa had rented six large suites for everyone. The suites centered around a tiny conference room so they could talk and get to know each other.

"You know," Saara said, "I got what I needed from this. All those pounds gone. You understand, right, Pipsqueak?"

"Sure," Pippa said in a flat voice. Of course she understood. Her family couldn't be bothered to spend more than twelve hours with her, and those under duress. She had tried to make everything right for them, tried to end the competition, tried to make them all try to see each other as siblings and maybe even as family.

Saara smiled at her—*beamed* at her, actually, with that megawatt S-Elf smile, the one that S-Elves rarely used on anyone in the North Pole. The magic didn't work on other mages, so it was a wasted smile, but it did make Saara look like she had stepped out of some kind of Christmas ad.

She set her package on top of Tahvo's, waved fingers in that little rolling gesture that she usually used when she said *Toodles,* which she, fortunately, didn't say, and then she put her finger alongside her nose, nodded, and vanished in a cascade of sparkling lights because—well, Saara had to outdo everyone else, even if they weren't here to see it.

Pippa threaded her fingers together, her stomach churning. She was not going to cry. She was not. Going to cry. Don't. Cry. Dammit.

The turn signal ticked. Pippa made herself look at Niko. His face, reflected in the rearview mirror, looked grim. His gaze didn't meet hers, which probably meant he was going to leave, too.

"As I see it," Joulu said from the row of seats behind Pippa, "we can go forth with your little adventure, or we can all go our separate ways."

Leave it to Joulu to state the obvious.

"You have somewhere you want to go?" Pippa asked, keeping her voice flat.

"Well, no, not really," Joulu said. "I really did clear my schedule. However, I do have friends I can visit here if we're not going to have family meetings."

He held up the package, tracing its cheap plastic side. Then he smiled at her.

The smile was gentle.

"I'll be honest with you," he said. "You were right. *This* looks like tons of fun. Since we're not doing the family thing, can I bring friends?"

Pippa shrugged. She had no idea that Joulu had friends in Las Vegas.

"Mortal friends?" she asked.

"Is there any other kind?" Joulu asked and laughed as if he had made some kind of joke, which she wasn't sure whether or not he had.

Pippa had no idea how to answer that. She couldn't even conceive of an answer because that would mean looking at her life and her friendships and what she wanted to do.

So, instead, she just gave Joulu a watery smile and turned away.

Niko pulled into the self-parking at the hotel and waved one of those cards the hotel had given them at check-in at the kiosk. Of course, it didn't work. Tahvo wasn't around to fix it.

Pippa was going to try hers when Niko punched a

button on the entry kiosk with his finger, almost as if he could stick his finger all the way through the kiosk, and a ticket came out. He held the ticket in his hand, waited until the liftgate went up, and then drove inside.

"Don't worry," he said to her. "They explained what to do if the card doesn't work."

Thank goodness he'd thought to ask. She wouldn't have. He drove up the different concrete floors, finally parking on the third floor near the stairs.

The three of them didn't even discuss it. They all knew that they'd have to take a lot of elevators here in Las Vegas—especially since their suite was on the thirty-fifth floor, which, the booking agent had told them (and so had the check-in clerk), was the lowest floor for a suite of that size.

Which they no longer needed.

"You two can go," Pippa said as Niko put the van in park. "I'll cancel everything. It's not a worry."

"I said I'm staying," Joulu said, sounding annoyed, as if she hadn't heard him at all.

But Niko remained horribly, awfully, terribly quiet.

"You have a family back in Chicago," Pippa said to him. "I'm sure you'd rather be with them."

He didn't move. Then his shoulders rose and fell in another sigh.

"I—we—me and Raine, we hoped that this would be..." He didn't finish the sentence. He didn't have to. They had hoped this would be some kind of fruitful family reunion, and he'd be back in the fold, exactly what Pippa had more or less promised him when she had asked him to come.

"I'm sorry," Pippa said.

"Yeah," Niko said. "Me too."

For a scary moment, she thought he was going to vanish as well, but he had flown here. He had plane tickets. And he had somehow rented this van.

"Let's get up to the room," he said. "Shall we?"

"I hope they have a landline—they have a landline, right?" Joulu asked. "I'd love to make some calls."

"Every hotel room has a landline," Niko said, but he sounded distant as if he was thinking of something else.

Pippa picked up the packets that Tahvo, Arja, and Saara had left behind and placed them with her own. Then she opened the sliding door on the side of the van and got out.

Joulu followed, clutching his. He took the extra packets off her pile.

"Friends, remember?" he said with a real smile. Everyone in the family had unusual beauty and charm with real smiles, and Joulu was the same.

"I know," Pippa said. "I understand."

She bit back everything else she thought of saying because what she wanted to say was angry and frustrated and she would take all of that out on Joulu. She'd say something like *friends are clearly more important than family*, but she didn't, she wouldn't, because that wasn't fair.

She and Joulu and Niko, they had all come here for a family thing, and there wasn't going to be a family thing, not like Pippa had planned.

She slammed the sliding door closed so hard that the van rocked. Then the doors locked, but there was no beep from the remote. Niko must have used an actual key.

Pippa walked around the back of the van, Joulu following. Niko waited near the stairs, holding his costume package casually in his right hand.

"Don't you think it's interesting," Niko said as he led the way to the stairs, "that our father wanted everyone to come here?"

"He didn't right away," Pippa said. "I had to explain a Santa run and how they were only held at Christmas time. I told him..." She paused and swallowed, not allowing her voice to break. "...that we'd be able to work on our differences, maybe figure out who wanted to succeed him the most."

"You said that?" Joulu said. "Who *wanted* to?"

"Yeah," Pippa said. "Why?"

Niko and Joulu exchanged glances as if they were co-conspirators.

"Think of the magic, Pippa," Niko said. "Our father's magic. The reason so many people get frustrated with him."

They had reached the top of the stairs. They were

concrete and boxed in, rather like Pippa felt. The air stank of gasoline trapped in that little box.

"Want," Joulu said into her silence. "Not need."

Because if it had been need, their father—their family—could have solved all of the world's problems. People needed food. They needed clothes. But sometimes—often—they wanted something else, something less necessary.

Even all those wishes for world peace that some older kids asked for, they didn't really want it. They couldn't imagine it. They were kindhearted souls who thought the world needed peace.

She put her hand on the metal railing. It was surprisingly cold, even though, by North Pole standards, Las Vegas wasn't cold at all. Mid-fifties Fahrenheit? That was downright balmy.

"I don't get it," Pippa said. "So I said 'want.' Big deal."

She started down the stairs. Niko followed, with Joulu right beside him, juggling the slippery costume packages.

"It might be a big deal to him," Niko said. "He told everyone to come."

"Except you and me," Pippa said.

"You were already coming," Niko said. "It was your idea. And I am no longer in the running for his job."

She stopped, and the other two almost walked into her. "You mean he turned this into a test?"

"Probably," Joulu said. "That's what he does."

"He contacted you, right?" Niko said.

"Oh, it was more casual than that," Joulu said. "It was

in passing. I saw him one afternoon, and he said, 'I trust you're going to Pippa's little race?'"

"*Little* race?" Pippa said, feeling even more annoyed.

"And I said that I wouldn't miss it, and he actually smiled at me and said, 'Good.'"

"That was it?" Niko asked.

"That was it," Joulu said. "As if he knew what I was going to do. But, then, he knows I like Las Vegas. I usually come here in January instead of going to Hawaii, much to Mom's dismay."

Pippa knew that, but she had never figured the reason Joulu was here was because the run was in Las Vegas. She had chosen to do this run instead of the myriads of other specialty races throughout the year because she knew a Santa run would give her family protective coloring. Some members were impossible to hide no matter what they did.

Like Arja, not that it mattered now.

Pippa took a deep breath and continued down the stairs. Her brothers followed, their boots thunking on the metal.

"A test," she muttered. "To see which one of us wanted it the most?"

"It's probably more complicated than that," Joulu said.

"Yeah." Niko's tone was decidedly dark. "It might even be as simple as trying to see who can follow orders."

"He can see that at the North Pole." Pippa stopped

on a landing to let some mortals go by. Four couples who looked at her curiously as she mentioned the North Pole.

"But there, everyone is supervised," Niko said. "When they're in the Greater World, they're not. They have to make choices for themselves."

Pippa sighed. Of course, their father would commandeer her plans for something of his own. For a *test*.

"So those three," she said, trying not to sound as disappointed as she felt, "they all passed, and we didn't."

"Well, the two of us," Joulu said and patted her on the shoulder. That made her jump. She couldn't remember the last time someone in her family had voluntarily touched her.

"Not necessarily," Niko said. "The Big Guy is tricky, remember? He might have something else in mind."

Those tears threatened again. Pippa didn't want to shed them. She didn't want to cry over any of this. And maybe tears weren't the appropriate response anyway. She was *angry* underneath it all. Everything she did was in service to her father or his agenda. Her job existed because of him. Her little house at the edge of Candy Cane Lane existed because of him.

Or, as he would say, because of his *position*. That was the important thing. The position.

No one cares who Santa Claus is, her father would say. *Just that he fulfills his duty each and every year.*

And that was where Niko had fought him. Niko had

said that their father wasn't doing his duty, that he was—in Greater World parlance—phoning it in.

Niko had challenged him, and Niko got banned.

She reached the bottom of the stairs and swiped at her face with the back of her hand. She was never very good at figuring out what to do next when plans changed. She liked schedules, which was why she was in charge of reviewing the schedules for each department.

The one thing she hadn't said to anyone was that she was busiest during January and February when the rest of her family was taking a well-deserved holiday. They always demanded that she go, and she did, but she worked through most of it.

Maybe she had figured that it served them all right to work while *she* was on holiday. The race had been for her as much as it had been for family unity.

Running had always been her thing. She had designed special boots so that she could run on the trails around the North Pole. She loved running in the ice and snow. Sometimes, she even ran in snowstorms. More than once, she'd been caught in a whiteout, yet she had always gotten home.

Maybe that was how she should think of this day. As a whiteout. No visible trails, so she couldn't follow what had been done before.

She was going to have to chart her own path.

"Pip," Niko said, concern in his voice. "You okay?"

She blinked and looked up at him. His stunning blue

eyes seemed concerned. The wrinkles on the side—laugh lines that everyone in the S-Elf line got when they hit adulthood—had become frown lines.

"You blanked out on us for a second," he said.

Joulu was peering at her as well. She wanted to think he looked concerned, too, but she wasn't going to let herself do that. She wasn't going to read anything into family interactions. Not anymore.

"Sorry," she said. "Just trying to figure out what to do next."

"Here's what I think," Joulu said in a much too cheerful voice. Had he put that on for her?

She couldn't tell.

"If you can, cancel the big suite and three of the suites. Keep the rest—one for you, one for me, and one for Niko and his whole family."

Niko held up his hands. "Joulu—"

"Let me finish," Joulu said. "I looked up this race. It's for *families*. Pippa was right to bring our family here so we could see families. But three bailed. That's on them. We're still a family, and I, for one, would love to get to know your wife and kids."

Niko's face flushed. He looked away, but not before Pippa saw tears glinting in his eyes.

"So what if you're no longer in the running for the Big Job?" Joulu said. "So what if you don't want to bring them to the North Pole? I wouldn't either. Those kids are part of the Greater World, too, and frankly, I think ruining the magic for them too early would be a mistake. So kudos to you."

"Bringing them to the North Pole would ruin the magic?" Pippa asked.

"You're seeing the sausage get made, my girl. It doesn't matter if it's magic. Who wants to watch those assembly lines or see that gigantic computer they're trying to rebuild belch angry smoke? I mean, come *on*."

She let out a small laugh.

Joulu slipped his arm around her waist and squeezed it.

"Hon, we have to stop focusing on whether or not we'll get the Big Job. Who cares, really? The Big Guy always said that no one cares who Santa Claus is. Maybe we should believe him, huh?"

Pippa looked at him.

"I mean," Joulu said. "Do *you* care who gets the job?"

"I think worrying about it is premature," she said in a very small voice. She had never expressed this opinion to anyone. Not to her siblings, not to her mother, and certainly not to her father.

"It's unseemly, isn't it?" Joulu said, pulling her tight for a moment and then letting her go. "I mean, it's like a monarchy or something, and we're all waiting for the king to die so we get all the power."

Her throat closed up, and all she could do was nod.

"You said it, not me." Niko sounded almost joyful. "Believe me, your life is a whole lot better if you stop focusing on whether or not you'll be the next Santa, and you use the powers you already have for good."

"So here's what I think," Joulu said. "We have Santa suits. We have our own little brand of joy, which is magic-powered. Let's spread it around."

"Without calling attention to ourselves," Niko said.

"Oh, heck, little brother," Joulu said. "This is Las Vegas. We can call attention to ourselves. That's one of the joys of this little town in the desert. *Everyone* is calling attention to themselves. No one will care about what we do, and if we do it right, we might actually make quite a few people smile."

Then he poked Pippa with his elbow, making her jump just a little.

"We start," Joulu said. "With Pippa. She needs a little joy."

"I'm okay," she said.

"Says the woman who's been crying off and on for the last hour." Joulu put his arm around her back again, and this time, he propelled her forward. "C'mon. Let's see what kind of Santa trouble we can get into."

She stumbled a little, then moved with him.

Niko had to walk fast to keep up. "I'm...um...I have a dilemma."

"Yes, yes, you have a family thing," Joulu said, almost dismissively.

"Well, that," Niko said. "I have to contact them and

see if Raine can rearrange the schedule. But, also, I'm known in charity circles."

"And that's a problem how?" Joulu said. "You've decided to come here to spread good cheer and participate in a charity run."

Niko still looked doubtful. Pippa put her hand on his arm.

"Maybe," she said, "you could talk to the people sponsoring the race. After it's done, of course. If you like what they're doing, then maybe do it in Chicago."

"In the middle of winter?" Niko said. "With the wind off the lake? No one would come."

"Maybe," Joulu said. "Or maybe they would see it as a lark. And don't call it a run because everyone would slip on the ice. But you could do a mile-long walk..."

Niko frowned. But it was a good frown. It was one of those thinking frowns that Pippa actually realized she had missed.

Then he smiled at Joulu. "I like that idea." Niko patted Joulu on the back, then started forward, stopping for only a second. "I really have to call my family."

"We'll meet you in your suite," Joulu said.

Niko half ran half walked down the wide sidewalk, heading to the ornate front of the building. He dodged cars with rideshare stickers and taxis and half a dozen people before Pippa looked away.

"You—I never realized how good you are at organizing," she said to Joulu.

"Oh, I have many talents unused by the family," Joulu said. "I've been told I have to apply to move from reindeer training to some higher position, and frankly, that sounds like too much work."

"I thought you liked the reindeer," Pippa said.

"I used to. But get bit enough times, and it gets old. Plus..." Joulu smiled. "They stink."

Pippa let out a surprised laugh.

"They do!" she said. "Only no one ever talks about it."

"No one ever talks about anything, darling," Joulu said. "At least, not in our family. No time is the excuse. Dealing with messy things like emotions, that's the real problem."

She looked at him. It was as if she had never seen Joulu before. Maybe she hadn't.

"Come on," he said. "We have negotiating to do. Time to turn on the S-Elf charm."

The charm, yes. She had forgotten. Joulu was right. They had a lot to do, and with a bit of charm and a touch of magic, they might be able to do it all.

THE
Santa
SERIES

Four

Anton tugged on the left sleeve of his white shirt, trying to hide the dots of chocolate shake that had stained it. He hadn't had time to change after hurrying home to drop Lila off with the housekeeper while he went to work.

He was at an early evening fundraiser for what he considered to be one of the most important charities in the business—the city's main food bank and hunger relief program. Fortunately, the fundraiser was casual. If it had been a black tie event, he would have had to be late.

But, fortunately, jeans and a white shirt seemed to be standard for several of the men here.

He had come with five of his charges—involuntarily retired with injuries, just like he had been. Only these five hadn't given any thought to saving or to learning how to budget, and they certainly hadn't figured out that charity was more than a needed tax deduction.

They had retired in Las Vegas, mostly because they had family here, and two had spent too much money on their new homes. Anton had tried not to roll his eyes as the two had told him about their choices. What could he say, after all? That they would regret it?

They would learn that soon enough.

The fundraiser was being held in a small ballroom donated by one of the Strip hotels on a slow evening. Weekdays after Thanksgiving were never very busy in Las Vegas. It got quieter and quieter here as December wore on until the craziness began right after Christmas.

Then, the locals avoided places like this as much as possible.

The ballroom was decorated in the hotel's signature black and gold. Anton stood near the open bar. He had already pointed out his five charges to the bartenders and told them to go easy. No cans, and after the first drink, everything should be watered-down.

He wasn't going to just teach these guys about finances. He was going to have to teach them how to be decent human beings.

Too many players got stuck in that superstar mentality because they had been receiving star treatment since they were in high school. A lot of players used that star treatment as an excuse to be their worst selves.

These guys weren't bad people, but they hadn't learned how to be good people either.

So, this fundraiser had two purposes. It was these five retired players' first introduction to charity, and it was going to be their first reminder that they were superstars no longer—especially since half the members of the retired players' board were here.

The board had retired players so famous that their names got said in the same hushed voice as some of the NBA superstars of today. Half of these guys had had big careers after their playing days, mostly in broadcasting. Some were here to coax the regular folks to bid on the silent auction items. Others had been invited to jack up the price per plate for attendance.

Anton had had his five buy their plates but at the lower end. He wanted them to know what it was like to sit in the back of the room and not on the dais.

Right now, he hung back with a glass of sparkling water and watched the poor young charges trying to work the room when there was no room to work.

"You are one nasty piece of work." Kwame Sutton stood beside him and grinned. "You're stealing from my playbook, you know."

"Always steal from the best, I say." Anton clinked his glass against Kwame's glass of sparkling water, nearly dislodging Kwame's tiny slice of lime.

Kwame was half a head shorter than Anton. He could get lost in a crowd of basketball players—which didn't bother him one bit. He was a sports junkie but had never been a player of any kind.

Two left feet, he'd said when Anton had asked. *Not to mention no balance and terrible eyesight.*

Kwame had turned his lack of prowess on any playing field into an advantage, though. He could talk sports, particularly statistics, and that had given him an edge with several franchises.

Years ago, Kwame had walked into some of the biggest venues in sports, demanded a meeting with the club president, and told them they had an obligation to teach their young players how to handle money.

He felt that the Rookie Transition Program, which consisted of days of lectures and warnings as well as guidelines, wasn't enough. He convinced several clubs to create financial literacy classes, which included full assignments and weeks of study.

Unfortunately, none of those clubs had made Kwame's classes mandatory. Anton had taken them when he was a young player because he knew his family knew nothing about money. The guys he had brought to this fundraiser had signed up for the classes but got distracted by all of the perks of their new job. *I meant to go* was the excuse that Anton heard the most when he talked to those forced to retire early.

"The difference is that I gave my guys something to aspire to," Kwame said. "You're teaching them where they stand post-career."

"Yeah," Anton said, letting his voice trail off. That was a big difference.

Kwame used to bring new players to fundraisers filled with famous players so that the new players would get their egos in check. Anton was bringing players who had received superstar treatment and needed to understand that they weren't that important anymore.

Still, Kwame had a slight smile on his face. "I hear Shaq will be DJ-ing later."

"That's another ticket," Anton said. "I didn't tell them about it, and it's sold out. Fortunately."

Fortunately, since the party charged $1000 per head just to get in the door, his guys could afford that now, but in the future, they'd regret spending that kind of money.

"You are brutal," Kwame said. "You know they'll want to go."

"Yep," Anton said, "and they won't be able to."

It was amazing how many doors closed once someone retired in the world of sports. That probably happened throughout life, but in sports, it happened early.

None of Anton's charges had turned thirty yet.

He felt a hundred years older than they were, even though he had maybe fifteen years on them.

"How's Lila holding up in the holidays?" Kwame asked, his voice lower than it had been. He was still staring at the party, people talking, mingling, laughing.

Anton watched as well, noting that his five players were standing near the front, clustered together.

He sighed at the thought of his daughter.

"I don't know how she's holding up, really," he said. "She's gotten really quiet. Her therapist says she's progressing nicely, but I have no idea what that means."

Kwame nodded, still not looking at him. Anton appreciated that. He had found that direct one-on-one conversations were hard about his daughter; he got too emotional too quickly.

"If only life were like basketball, right?" Kwame said. "You know where you stand in a game, how many fouls you've made, what you've done right, and what you've done wrong, and how hard you have to work to fix it."

"Or if you can fix it at all," Anton said, thinking of his leg. "I guess life is like basketball in that."

"Yeah, maybe." Kwame sipped his water and looked like he was about to plunge into the crowd.

But Anton wasn't ready to let him go just yet.

"I signed us up for the Run On Santa Claus Lane," he said. "I'm hoping it'll make her smile just a little."

Kwame glanced over at him. "I thought you weren't going to do anything athletic with her."

"I signed us up for the mile walk," Anton said. "It's not timed."

And he wasn't sure he could make it farther than that. His leg was already aching from standing on it just this short period of time.

"She may not like it," Kwame said. "Some people don't like crowds."

That sounded like a personal truth. Anton raised his eyebrows just a little. He hadn't considered that. She'd clung to him at the packet pickup. How would she be in a sea of Santas?

"I've done it a couple of times," Kwame said. "It can be overwhelming."

Anton hadn't even thought of that.

"Make sure you have something on her that's identifiable in case she does get separated from you," Kwame said.

Now, Anton was worried that he had made the wrong choice. "What do you mean?"

"I went a few years ago and saw a high-energy three-year-old girl whose parents had dressed her like a little green elf. I thought it was weird until I followed them down the street. She was always running away from them, but they could see her, this dot of green in a sea of red."

One more thing to consider. Anton sighed. "I'll talk to Lila. Maybe we'll get her a hat or something. Even though I doubt she'll leave my side."

But he knew as well—or maybe better—than Kwame that kids surprised you.

It was too late to back out. And besides, he'd been telling Lila that the only way to get through was to keep showing up. He hadn't consulted the therapist on that. He had a hunch she would advocate letting his kid pick and choose what she did.

But eight was a little young to be in charge of the family's schedule, at least in Anton's opinion. He would decide what they did and didn't do, but he would listen to her. If she didn't like something, they probably wouldn't do it again.

Kwame did not respond to that. In fact, the silence got long and a bit stressful.

Finally, Kwame pointed toward the stage near the front of the ballroom.

"I," he said a little dramatically, "have networking to do. Good luck with your humility lessons."

For a moment, Anton thought that Kwame meant him. Anton thought he was humble enough, but maybe he wasn't. Maybe he was doing things wrong with his daughter. Then, Anton realized that Kwame meant his five charges, not Anton himself.

Humility lessons. He supposed that was what it all was. Those brutal reminders that life never ever went as expected, no matter how much you wanted it to.

He had one of the bartenders top off his drink, then headed into the crowd himself. Time to work with his guys and ease them into their future, whether they liked it or not.

THE
Santa
SERIES

The Santa suits were terribly cheap. They were so thin that Pippa figured she could poke her fingernail into a sleeve and make a hole with very little effort.

She didn't test it. But she did run her finger along the red surface, and noted that the red dye stained her skin.

"What were you expecting?" Joulu asked. He was standing in the living room of her suite.

The nice thing about this suite was that it had a view of the mountains that ringed the city. She hadn't been aware that mountains could be several shades of brown, with a touch of snow on the top. They looked almost like the paintings that graced the walls.

"I mean," Joulu said, "they *give* you the suit. They probably had to buy in bulk."

She peered at him. He was holding up the coat of his suit, the Santa hat already on his head. The hat made his blond hair look white. He looked like a live-action movie Santa before the beard.

Which, in some ways, he was.

He flicked the coat as if it were a cape in front of a bull. Little fuzzy red balls floated in the air. He laughed.

He had taken the package apart in her room, commenting on each piece—the pants that looked too small to fit anyone, the shiny—and thin—plastic belt, the hat and coat, and surprisingly, a fluffy white beard that appeared to be made of angel hair.

It wasn't. Angel hair would have cut the skin. But the beard looked almost real.

She didn't want Joulu to put it on and complete the illusion. She knew all the S-Elves had a resemblance to the Big Guy. She just didn't want to see it on her older brother—or on herself.

Niko wasn't in the suite. He had gone to the airport in some kind of shuttle, because he didn't want to risk driving the van more than necessary. Pippa was trying to get him to return it. Joulu agreed, saying they could take rideshares everywhere. But Pippa had a hunch that Niko wanted the van and the freedom it would provide him for his family.

She also had a hunch that Raine would be driving from now on.

"We could magic these, I suppose," Pippa said. She

was trying to imagine what everyone at the North Pole would say if they saw photos of these horrid costumes. All right, really, she was trying to imagine what her father would say.

He always stressed that they needed the best of everything, and this clearly wasn't the best. It was damn close to making a mockery of her father's annual costume.

"Oh," Joulu said. "That would ruin the fun. If we do anything, we make it our own with Greater World supplies. Glitter or rhinestones or, I don't know, holiday bows from packages."

She smiled in spite of herself, imagining them working on the costumes until the wee hours.

"What are your friends doing?" she asked.

"Meeting me here tonight for drinks. You want to join?"

The last thing she needed was to be a third, or fifth, or seventh wheel. She shook her head.

"I meant about the costume," she said.

"Oh, my friends will make it their own. One is wearing a black tutu instead of the pants. Another one is going to put spangles all over the hat. Another says he's going to surprise us, which leads me to believe he'll Krampus or Grinch it or something."

"You can do that?" she asked, thinking those images would ruin the run.

"You haven't looked at all of the online pictures of this

run, have you?" Joulu asked. "Tahvo showed me before we left the North Pole. He thought this was all very unserious. I *well*, *duh*'ed him, and he got quite offended. Our brother is too serious."

"I've noticed that," Pippa said tightly. She didn't want to discuss Tahvo. She was deeply angry at him. If he hadn't said he had something more important to do, then maybe all five of her siblings would still be here.

"Oh, forgive him, girl," Joulu said as if he could read her mind. Maybe he could. There were rumors that mind-reading was a skill some S-Elves had. "He really does have an important job."

"Yes, he does, but he agreed, and the Big Guy said he could come."

"Doesn't make his job any less important," Joulu said. "It certainly is more important than training reindeer or checking schedules. Or is that checking them *twice*?"

"Actually," Pippa said. "My job is really important. If we don't follow the schedules to the letter, then we miss all of the December deadlines."

Joulu looked at her over the bright red coat. Its maraschino-cherry-red color accented the maraschino-cherry-red color of his cheeks and made his blue eyes even bluer.

"Honey," he said, "we need to get you to de-stress. Relax. Have fun. It was your idea to do this for fun, right?"

"No," she said before she could stop the word. "I wanted to unite our family."

"Well, you're uniting the three of us, and we're going to get to know Niko's family. So take the win. And have fun. You're going to run downtown Las Vegas with five thousand Santas."

"Five thousand *fake* Santas."

"Can you actually imagine five thousand *real* Santas?" Joulu pulled the coat over his head. "God forbid."

She let out a tiny laugh despite herself. That had happened a few other times around Joulu now. She hadn't realized how funny he was. He always seemed so serious up North.

She liked this side of him.

"So we shouldn't magic these or maybe bring some of our own suits?"

"Oh, darling." He set the coat on the back of a light blue chair. She had a feeling that the red dye would rub off. At least the family could afford to pay damages. "Our suits would kill us. They're designed for the cold. This city is *not* cold."

True enough.

"I think Niko wanted us to go around in the suits and visit charities or something," Pippa said. "I'm not sure my suit will last more than one use."

"Pips," Joule said, "you need to *relax*."

She let out a sigh. "I don't know how to relax, Joulu. I don't think I ever have."

He tossed the beard on top of the suit jacket and walked over to her, grabbing both of her arms and making her face him. He peered into her eyes as if he could see deep into her soul and then said, "Yep, you're right. You've not relaxed a single day in your life."

She laughed, but the laugh was nervous.

"You," he said, turning her toward the door, "need to meet someone outside of the family. I'm ordering you to go downstairs and sit in that fancy bar that spills into the atrium. *Talk* to people. I promise they'll be interesting."

Then he pushed her forward.

"A bar?" she asked. "I've heard bad things about meeting people in bars."

"Oh, for goodness' sake, darling. I'm not saying that you should marry them. *Talk* to them. Talk, talk, talk."

He propelled her all the way to the door, then he pulled it open, handed her one of those key cards, the purse that she had to carry in the Greater World, and shoved her into the hallway.

She stood there, a little confused, and turned toward him. He blocked the doorway with his body, extending both arms to each side.

He grinned at her, let go of the door frame with his right hand and waggled the fingers. "Toodles, as our oh-so-lovely sister Saara would say."

Then he closed the door. Tightly. With authority.

As if it were his room and not hers.

Pippa felt a moment of irritation, which then turned

into amusement. He had just made fun of Saara. Did that mean he really didn't like her either?

Pippa might have to ask...after she spent the requisite time in the bar, whatever that would be.

Six

Anton sat on a too-soft chair-stool in the atrium bar at the newest, most expensive hotel on the Las Vegas Strip. His seat gave him the advantage of being able to see the elevators as well as anyone entering the atrium bar from the tower floors.

He was nursing a Diet Coke, even though he didn't really like it. He'd had the bartender add a touch of lemon on the side, so the damn thing looked like a real drink. He was trying to prevent any criticism from coming his way, and he knew there would be a lot.

His mother had arrived just this morning.

Darling, she'd said in that breezy tone she used when she was lying. *Only here for a few hours with a friend, and then I'm heading to LA for a week or so before heading to Paris for the holiday.*

Of course, she didn't invite him to come, but she would call him if she got stranded by the current boyfriend, which had happened far too many times. She used to trade on the fact that she was NBA star Anton Walker's mother, but that cachet had faded over time, which she loudly complained about.

Most of the players of your caliber become movie stars after they retire, she would say. Or she would mention being a broadcast announcer—anything to keep Anton in the public eye so that she could piggyback off his fame.

Anton had made the mistake of talking to the front desk after coming down from the thirtieth-floor suite where his mother was staying. His mother's current lover was off on some golfing adventure this afternoon. Anton had gone up with Lila, holding her hand, ready to yank her out of there if the boyfriend was anywhere nearby.

He wasn't, which brought Anton some relief, but not enough. And then he had gone to the desk to ask when his mother had checked in.

A week ago, of course. *She spent Thanksgiving with us*, the desk clerk had said with a smile. The hotel was still trying to promote all of its features to get new clients because there was so much competition.

Anton had managed to sound calm when he thanked the clerk and headed into the bar.

She was here one whole week, and his mother couldn't be bothered to even call. She *knew* her granddaughter had lost her own mother not even three months before, and maybe, just maybe, her granddaughter might've appreciated a little love from her other grandmother—*his* mother.

But that woman wasn't capable of love.

He felt odd leaving Lila with her for even two hours. She had told him to drive off and have some adventure as if he were still a young man with a fancy car that might impress the people at valet parking.

But he knew better. He was waiting for Lila to come back down, alone, most likely, and possibly in tears, because that was often how things ended when his mother was around.

He had an hour to decide whether or not to bring his daughter here, and he would have decided against it if he hadn't been talking to her on speaker and Lila hadn't wandered into the room.

I'll go, Lila had said. *I don't mind.*

Unfortunately, she had said that loud enough that his mother had heard.

It's settled, then. See you soon, his mother had said and hung up before he could think of a way to get them all out of this.

So, he was sitting alone at a glass bar designed by someone famous enough to have signed the damn thing and have his name plastered all over the promotion for the atrium bar. *With a glass bar specially designed by...*

And Anton had looked away. He really didn't care— not about any of it. The trappings of wealth had lost their meaning to him in his second year as a player; after witnessing the same behavior he had observed at UConn, where he had attended on a basketball scholarship. It didn't matter how rich people were. They could be nice, or they could be assholes, and the money only enhanced both traits.

The elevator for the tower rooms opened, and a blonde woman got out. She looked vaguely familiar, but he couldn't place her. She was thin but not that tall. Her blonde hair was cut in a wedge against her shapely skull.

He wasn't even sure if he should call her a blonde since her hair was the color of winter wheat. He had never seen that color outside of a bottle, and now he'd seen it a couple of times in one week.

There had been that blond family who had acted like idiots at packet pickup...

He frowned at her, wondering if she was one of them. He couldn't tell. She certainly wasn't one of the assholes who had snapped at the volunteers, nor was she the woman who stood to one side, meaty arms crossed.

So, probably not. He was probably just aware of the color, having associated it with bad behavior a few days before.

This woman stopped at the edge of the faint blue, gold, and white carpet that made the atrium bar look like it had risen from a foamy sea. She seemed doubtful as if she wasn't even sure she wanted to come inside.

She scanned the handful of people scattered around

the bar in the early afternoon. When her gaze landed on him, his heart rate inexplicably rose.

He told himself it was only because he was agitated about his mother and Lila. Still, he smiled at the woman because she looked as uncomfortable as he felt.

She squared her shoulders and walked across that carpet, dodging the glass tables. They had etchings along the side and were probably designed by the same person who had designed the bar.

She reached his little section of the bar, and that little uplift her look had given his heart turned into a sinking feeling.

She recognized him. He hadn't had to deal with many basketball groupies since he retired, but those he did have to deal with would stick to him until he had to rudely shake them off.

He looked down at his Diet Coke. He hadn't even taken a single sip.

She sat one seat away from him, a typical groupie move meaning, *I'm not really that interested*, when in fact they were. He spun the glass around.

He'd spoken to this bartender, too, when he'd first sat down and said he didn't want the can. If his mom brought Lila down—and of course, she wouldn't unless he wasn't expecting her—his mom would ask why he wasn't drinking *real* alcohol if she saw the Diet Coke can. He just didn't want to have that discussion.

He hadn't really realized until just today how much of his behavior around his mother was geared toward avoiding her cutting comments.

And he had subjected Lila to that when she was the most vulnerable.

But he had to trust her. She said she'd make an excuse and leave if she didn't want to be there. Her relationship with her grandmother would be different than his with his mother, just by definition. He'd learned that with his own grandfather, who had sat quietly during Anton's high school games, looking on with something akin to joy.

Apparently, he had criticized Anton's father terribly throughout *his* short basketball career, and that had made Anton's father want to stay as far from sports as possible.

Some people learned and improved. And then there was his mother, the kind of person who learned the wrong thing from every lesson.

Something white floated at the edge of his eyesight, and before he could think the better of it, he looked.

The blond was reading the drink menu as if she was going to be tested on it. Her mouth, which looked oddly like a bow, was pulled tight, and she had the smallest frown he'd ever seen.

"Do you have something peppermint?" she asked. She had a slight accent. It sounded European, but he couldn't place it, which bothered him. Usually, Anton was good at identifying accents.

"A lot," the bartender said, his back to her. "It's the holiday season, and our mixologist went crazy with the peppermint schnapps."

"What's that?" she asked, which really got Anton's attention. She almost looked like a child trying to figure out what candy to try.

He had to say something in spite of himself.

"You don't want peppermint schnapps," he said.

The bartender gave him a sideways smile without turning around.

The woman looked over at Anton. She had the brightest blue eyes he had ever seen. And her cheeks were a dusty rose, something he'd never seen outside of a painting.

Her features were delicate and very old-fashioned. If she'd had a slightly curly hairstyle, she could have stepped out of a silent movie—maybe even given Mary Pickford a run for her money.

"Why?" the woman asked, and she sounded genuine.

"It's sweet," he said. "It tastes like candy. And if you drink too much of it, you'll be sick for days."

"Oh." She set the menu down. "I can't be sick, not right now."

Did anyone ever have time to get sick? he almost asked and then stopped himself. He didn't want to engage. Besides, he wasn't sure if that was flirty or passive-aggressive. His mother brought out the worst in him.

But for the moment he had talked to the woman, he hadn't thought about his mother or worried about Lila.

"What are you drinking?" the woman asked him.

"Just a Diet Coke," he said, sounding almost apologetic.

"Well, I know what that is," she said. "I'll have one too."

The bartender gave him another look, then grabbed a can of Diet Coke from one of several tiny refrigerators in the center island.

The bartender poured some liquid out of the can over ice, then pushed the glass toward the woman, setting the can on the side, like he was supposed to do.

"You finish yours already?" she asked Anton, nodding toward the can.

"Um." He wasn't sure how to answer her. If he said yes, he was lying. If he said no, he would have to explain about his mother, and he wasn't sure he wanted to do that.

"Sorry," the woman said, waving her hand. "I'm being too talkative. My brother told me to come down here and talk to people. I think he must've thought the place would be packed or something."

"Why would he want you to talk to people?" Anton asked, then mentally kicked himself. For a man who didn't want to get drawn into a conversation, he was participating rather well.

"He says I don't know anyone outside the family."

She took the glass from the bartender and then spun it toward him. "My friend here has a lemon. Can I get one?"

The bartender reached into a little tray of cut-up fruit, grabbed a lemon slice by its rind, and set it on the glass.

"There," she said. "At least it looks right now."

It didn't, but Anton didn't say that. He couldn't help himself. He was curious now.

"How can you not know anyone outside of your family?" he asked. He almost asked something insensitive like *Are you some kind of shut-in,* or *did you belong to a cult,* or *is there a family compound I should be worried about?* Not that what he did was sensitive. He was a little too astonished, maybe even a tad judgmental.

But the woman didn't seem to notice.

"I don't think he meant that literally," she said, then frowned as if considering it. "Although maybe he does. I have friends who aren't part of my family. I just don't...see them that often."

Her shoulders slumped.

"Maybe he has a point," she said more to herself than to Anton. Then she straightened and smiled at him.

Her smile was the brightest smile he'd ever seen. He was amazed the bartender didn't stagger backward from its power. Anton felt it viscerally as if the smile had the power to pull him forward.

Maybe it did. He was leaning toward her now, which might've seemed a bit creepy.

He made himself sit up so that it didn't look like he was drawn to her.

"I mean," she was saying, "I do work for the family business, and I hardly ever leave home, except in the offseason, and then I go on races, and I don't really talk to anyone."

"Races?" Anton asked. He was fully committed to the conversation now. There was no backing out.

"Oh, I'm not good or anything. I just like to challenge myself." She smiled again, but this one was self-deprecating and didn't have the wattage.

"What kind of races?" he asked.

"Oh, running," she said. "I'm here for the Run On Santa Claus Lane."

And surprisingly, the smile left her face. He would have thought that the Run On Santa Claus Lane would make anyone smile, but apparently not. These last few days had shown him that he was making countless incorrect assumptions.

"You don't look excited about it," he said.

She shrugged one shoulder and pushed at the can of Diet Coke hard enough to nearly make it topple. She caught it with her hand, then put both hands in her lap.

"I was," she said, "but then...reality, you know."

"No, I don't. What happened?"

"Oh." She looked down at those hands. "I had thought maybe my family could join me. They'd get to see how much fun the races are and what I'm like when I'm not at home. But, no. It didn't work out. They went home."

Now he knew who she was. She was the woman who had apologized for the blond jerks at packet pickup.

"They went *home*?" he asked. "But didn't you just say your brother told you to come down here?"

She shrugged and dipped her head just a little. "Two of my brothers stayed. Everyone else left, they acted like I'd been holding them prisoner or something."

Her voice was barely above a whisper.

"It was a mistake, bringing them here, it was a mistake, and I should've known that, and I have no idea why I think anything with my family will work out."

Then she raised her head and saw him. Her cheeks flooded with red, which made her eyes seem even brighter. Or maybe that was the tears floating in them.

"Sorry," she said. "You didn't need this."

"Oh," Anton said. "Maybe I did."

Because he had to remember that everyone had family issues and a bit of compassion went a long way. It was certainly a lesson he could bring to his charges and maybe take in some of that for himself as well. After all, his mother had her own challenges growing up. It didn't forgive her behavior, but it might explain some of it.

"Well," the woman said, "bearing your soul to a stranger in a bar. How much more clichéd can you get?"

"Maybe that was what your brother wanted you to do," Anton said.

"Yeah, maybe," she said with just a bit of bitterness. "Or maybe he wanted me out of the room." Then she laughed once, without humor. "Even though it was my room."

Anton didn't know what to say to that. He had no idea how to respond to this beautiful, sad woman. Should he tell her that he had seen one of her brothers acting like an ass at packet pickup? Or maintain his silence?

He was saved from saying anything because the elevator door opened, and his mother got out. She was tall and thin, her muscular legs visible beneath a pair of unseasonal shorts. She had Lila by the shoulder, pulling her forward. Lila was trying to shake her off, but not managing.

Anton got up to head toward them, but his mother only sped up. She banged Lila against one of the glass tables so hard that it rang like a bell.

"Mother!" he said in his most commanding voice. "Let her go."

His mother pushed Lila forward. Lila stumbled toward him, then wrapped her arms around him so tightly that it hurt.

"This child," his mother said, "is the rudest creature I have ever encountered. She acts like she's the Lord Almighty, ready to pass judgment on all of us."

"Mother," he said, feeling both angry and helpless. He had subjected his child to this. He should have known better.

The beautiful woman slid off her stool and leaned on it. The other patrons in the atrium bar were watching as well.

"She acted like I'm some kind of witch," his mother said. "She said that her real grandmother treats her kindly and actually cares about her. *I* care, Anton, and I will *not* be in competition with a woman whose daughter prostituted herself to get herself a pro basketball player—"

"Shut up!" Lila shouted. She let go of Anton and took a step forward, her hands in fists. "That's my *mother* you're talking about."

"Well, you're better off—"

"Don't you dare finish that sentence." Anton placed himself between his mother and his daughter. "I brought her here against my better judgment, thinking maybe she needed some kind of relationship with you. I was wrong, and I'm going to need to make that up to my little girl. You—"

"I'm her grandmother," his mother said. "I deserve—"

"You don't deserve anything," Anton said. "And as of now, you're absolved of grandparent duties. Stay away from my daughter. We want nothing to do with you."

His mother straightened. She had gone gray beneath her perfect makeup.

"What?" she said. He recognized the tone. It was too calm. It was her *You thought I was mad before? You thought wrong* tone. She was about to level up, and that would be even uglier.

"You heard me," he said. "Now, get away from my daughter."

His mother didn't listen. She came forward, and so did he. He noted out of the corner of his eye that the largest bartender had come around the front of the bar, probably to prevent a physical altercation.

"She's my granddaughter," his mother said.

But he wasn't going to let her continue. "No, she's not," he said. "Not anymore. In fact, you can lose my number as well. Neither of us ever want to see you again."

"Now, Tone," she said, using the stupid nickname she'd given him years ago, "you don't mean that."

"I mean every word," he said. Then he waved his hand at the bar. "And there are witnesses. If that's not good enough for you, you can talk to my lawyer."

"Baby, your lawyer doesn't like me," she said. "When I call him—"

For money, Anton mentally added.

"—he won't give you a message."

"Yeah," Anton said. "He told me to cut you off years ago. I'm finally listening to him."

His mother stood before him, her mouth slightly open. She tilted her head as if she couldn't believe what she was hearing.

"Baby," she said.

"You can leave now," he said.

"I'm the one staying in the hotel," she said. "I'm the one—"

"Then go back to your room, Mother," he said. "Get away from my daughter."

The bartender had moved closer. After Anton said that, the bartender put a hand on her arm.

She screeched and shook him off. "You can't touch me," she said.

"Ma'am," he said. "I think you should listen to your son. It's time to go back to your room."

"You can't talk to me like that," she said. "I'll have your job."

"Ma'am." His voice was low but forceful. "I know who your son is, and so does the whole city. We have security cameras. If you want to fight this, then the footage will be given to the police and any other interested parties."

"You can't let him talk to me like this," she said to Anton.

But Anton stayed silent, his hands behind him, holding Lila in place.

"The entire bar saw how poorly you treated that child, ma'am," the bartender said. "And we have a video of it. I'm pretty sure that would be enough for a restraining order against you."

And the bartender looked at Anton, who nodded, feeling a bit lightheaded now that he had vented decades of anger in this stupid glass bar in front of one of the prettiest women he'd ever seen.

She was leaning on the stool, not looking at him or his

mother but at Lila. It seemed like the woman was sending warmth toward Lila, although he wasn't sure how he knew that or if his feeling was even accurate.

He couldn't look at the woman any longer, though, because his mother was still commanding the attention of the room.

"Anton wouldn't do something like that," his mother said.

"I will now," Anton said, then bowed his head at the bartender. "Thank you."

"Our pleasure, sir," the bartender said. "Ma'am, please return to your room, or I will have security escort you."

"I am not in the wrong here," she said. "This is *my* granddaughter—"

"And if my mother treated my daughter that way," the bartender said, "I would make sure my daughter never saw her again either."

"You people just support him because he's a celebrity," his mother said bitterly.

"Believe what you want, ma'am," the bartender said. "Just get out of the bar."

She looked at Anton as if she expected him to defend her. He had done that too many times. Or he had been the one to escort her back to her room. Or he had found a way to get her out of trouble, because, he had rationalized everything because she was his mother.

He was partly responsible for creating those expectations, but they stopped now, because they threatened his daughter.

"Fine," his mother said. "Just fine. Fine." She backed up, hitting one of the chairs near a glass table. Then she moved around it. "You won't see me again, and you'll miss me. That little girl won't get the benefit—"

"Don't talk about my daughter," Anton growled.

"Fine." His mother spit the word. "You'll regret this, Anton."

"You're right," he said, and she stopped backing up, hope lighting up her eyes. "I regret that I didn't do something sooner. I should have cut you off years ago."

"You *bastard*!" she said.

"You would know," he said.

She looked at him in shock, and this time, when the bartender took her arm, she didn't shake him off. She let him lead her to the elevators. She got on, and kept her back to the bar as the doors closed.

Anton let out a breath, then turned around, expecting to see his daughter in tears. Instead, her eyes were filled with fury.

"Are you all right?" he asked.

"She's a horrible person," Lila said.

"Yeah." He spoke softly. "I'm sorry. I thought...I don't know what I thought. Maybe she'd be different with you. She—"

"She said terrible things about my mom," Lila said. "She said worse things about you. And I'm sorry, Dad. I had to tell her that she was mean, and that's when she grabbed me."

"Let me see your arm," he said, afraid she was bruised.

"I'm okay," Lila said. "Really. But I don't want to see her again."

"You won't," he said. "I promise."

"Good." Lila looked fierce. He was proud of her and just a little relieved. Her therapist had said that she had to let some of the anger out, and this incident had done that, if nothing else.

He stroked her hair, and wished to hell he had better judgment. He mentally promised himself he would do better.

"Let me settle up," he said, "and then we can go."

Lila nodded. She hadn't moved from her spot near his chair-stool. She was clinging to the back of it, almost as if it were a lifeline.

He went around her to the bar. The bartender moved closer to him.

"The lady over there already paid, sir," he said, nodding toward the beautiful woman.

She was still standing beside her chair. She gave him a tiny smile.

"I figured you didn't need more to do," she said.

He smiled at her. He had learned long ago that when someone did something nice, you didn't fight over it. You simply said thank you, which he did.

She nodded.

He turned back to the bartender. "We'll get out of your way," he said.

"All right," the bartender said. "And don't worry, sir, we'll deep-six the security footage."

"I'd rather you wouldn't." He reached into his pocket, removed his wallet, and took out a business card. "Please send it to my lawyer."

The bartender took the card. "I can't do that, sir, but I'll let the bosses know. It's better if you have your lawyer contact us. Maybe within the hour."

"Got it," Anton said and tapped his wallet on the bar. "Thank you."

He put his arm around Lila and carefully steered them through the maze of glass tables.

"Those people were really nice," Lila said.

"The bartenders?" Anton asked as he stepped off that hideous carpet. He couldn't help himself. He gave the elevator one last look. He hoped he wouldn't have to return to this hotel for a long time.

"And that lady," she said. "She was nice."

"She was," Anton said.

"And pretty," Lila said.

Anton gave her a sideways glance. Apparently, Lila didn't recognize the woman from that packet pickup. Nor was Lila objecting to the fact the lady was white.

"Yes," Anton said. "She's pretty."

"She liked you, Dad," Lila said.

A change of subject. Maybe that was good. Maybe it

wasn't. He sure as hell wished that he had some kind of manual so he knew if what he was doing was right.

"Sometimes people are kind without an ulterior motive," he said and realized just how pompous he sounded.

"Oh, I know," Lila said, apparently not noticing the pomposity. She moved out of his grasp, then checked the elevators as well, as if to see if his mother was returning.

She wasn't. The elevator doors remained closed.

She liked you, Dad, Lila said of that pretty woman. And he had liked her. He wanted to go back and say, *See? We all have difficult families*, but he didn't. He probably wouldn't even see her again.

A hotel guest in a fancy hotel, down at the bar for a moment because her brother had sent her there. A hotel that Anton wasn't going to go to again unless he had to be there for some charity event.

That woman was a stranger to the town and to him. He was oddly sad that he wouldn't see her again, but it was one of those chance encounters.

Maybe talking with her about her family had given him the courage to take on his.

Or maybe, seeing how his mother had treated Lila had brought it all home. He could feel that grip on his own shoulder. His mother had dragged him all over town as a child, complaining about his behavior and making sure they never went back to places where he had embarrassed her.

Sometimes it was amazing that anyone grew up unscarred at all.

He lowered his hand so that he could take his daughter's. She slipped her hand in his. She hadn't let him do that before, calling it a "baby" move. But she didn't seem to mind right now.

His mother had caused more turmoil than she knew.

He had no idea how he would make it up to Lila, but somehow, he would.

Seven

Pippa watched them leave the bar. The man—Anton?—was tall. His mother had called him a celebrity and one of the bartenders had said that they watched him play over the years. So, probably basketball, given his height.

His daughter was going to be tall, too, and his mother had been tall. That woman was an awful piece of work. It had taken all of Pippa's self-control not to zap her.

The family didn't zap very often, but they did sometimes, making a person feel like they'd put their hand in a light socket just to stop certain terrible behaviors.

It was one of the few weird S-Elf skills that Pippa had thought there was no use for—until she saw that hideous woman banging her grandchild around like the girl was the ball in a pinball machine.

Pippa let out a breath, then climbed back onto the chair-stool. The Diet Coke didn't interest her as much, but she sipped it anyway.

Her heart was pounding. That was the most drama she had seen in months, maybe even years.

Maybe Joulu was right. Maybe she did need to get out more.

Maybe then she wouldn't think every man she met was good-looking. Not that she was having that thought about every man around her. But wow, Anton had been. Dark brown eyes filled with compassion, a deep voice, and the way he had protected his daughter...

Pippa was mesmerized by that entire drama, even though she felt like some rude stalker staring at a slow-moving accident.

She tried to do what she could. She sent as much magical warmth to the daughter as she could without actually stepping in even though she wanted to. She wanted to protect that girl just like Anton had.

They were handling it, though. Who knew that such a well-dressed, handsome man, nursing a drink alone in this strange bar in the middle of the afternoon, had real problems—and such a horrible mother?.

Pippa shuddered. At least her mother was nice. Maybe too nice. Maybe too much of a pushover.

Her father was sharp-tongued and a bit self-centered (*A bit?* a voice that sounded like Joulu said in her head), but he was nothing like that woman. Some of her siblings were difficult, but she couldn't imagine any of them treating a child like that.

The entire family was about treating children well.

Maybe she should have approached her family that way instead of trying to bond with them as a unit. Maybe she should have said that they needed to see children in their native environment.

But that might've caused other issues. Niko had wanted the entire family to see how many children were missed by Santa every year, and that still got everyone's back up at the North Pole. Some people wouldn't even allow anyone to say Niko's name.

She hadn't told him that. He seemed calmer now that the other three were gone. Maybe they had treated him badly, too.

She took the final sip from her glass of Diet Coke. She peered suspiciously at the can, then shook her head. She'd had enough.

She'd come down here. She'd talked with someone she didn't know. She'd seen some pretty amazing drama.

She wanted to say that it had given her perspective— and maybe it had. Just enough to realize that everyone had family issues, some worse than others.

Maybe she had known that, but maybe she hadn't, not on a deep level.

She left an extra tip on the bar because those bartenders deserved it after the afternoon they'd had.

Then she went back up to her room to think about everything she had seen.

THE
Santa
SERIES

Anton was furious. On the drive home, he thought about calling Lila's therapist for her take on what to do next, but he didn't need the therapist. Not really. He knew what to do, and better yet, he had already done it.

He had defended his daughter, and he had banned his mother from their lives for good.

He would have to call his attorney, though, and formalize all of this.

The guard at the security building for the gated community he lived in waved his brand-new Lexus SUV through with a smile. Anton made himself smile back.

He drove along the windy road to his oversized house, which his mother (who had never been here) would have called a mansion before she demanded a piece of it. The house was two-story, light brown, with desert landscaping. It was on a hillside which overlooked the entire Vegas Valley.

Both he and Lila loved standing on the back patio—if something that large could be called a patio—and looking at the ever-changing lights twinkling below.

He pulled into the driveway but kept the garage door down. He had to go out again later for another charity event—damn December—but he might cancel out or see if one of his associates could take over for him.

It all depended on Lila.

She was sitting quietly next to him, her hands resting on top of her bright pink backpack. Unlike the backpacks the other girls at her school carried, Lila's was not decorated with a cartoon figure, nor did it have little stuffed animals hanging off of it.

She had picked out the plainest pack she could find, and when he asked her about it, she said she'd wait to see what the cool kids carried.

She now knew, but that hadn't changed her behavior.

He turned to her, about to apologize for the umpteenth time, when Lila said, "What's wrong with her?"

"My mother?" he said, startled. He had expected the discussion, if it was going to come, to start once they were in the cavernous kitchen.

"Who else?" Somewhere, his beautiful daughter had learned how to deploy sarcasm like a master. Probably from Cherise, who used to barrage him with sarcasm once she realized that her pregnancy ploy would get her a home and child support for the rest of her life, but not marriage to a famous basketball player.

"I don't know," he said, shaking his head. "She's been like that my whole life."

"And you thought I'd *enjoy* spending time with her?" Lila's hand went to her shoulder. It was probably sore. He was going to have to look at it.

"I didn't..." he stopped himself and sighed. "Look, my grandfather—my father's father, was supposed to have been very mean to my dad, but he was great with me. He came to all my games, had nothing but positive to say, and was someone I could lean on when my mother acted... well, like she did today. I guess I hoped that she would change like that too, with her granddaughter."

"Well, she didn't." Lila smoothed the surface of the backpack. "That was awful."

"I know," he said. "I'm sorry."

Then Lila peered at him. "You *lived* with her?"

"Eighteen years," he said. "Although, to be fair, I spent most of my teen years avoiding her."

He tried out for every single sport he could, starting when he was ten. He was gone from home most of the time. His grandfather had driven him to a lot of those early games.

"I can see why." Lila reached for the door handle, then stopped. She frowned at him, and he braced himself.

Whatever she was going to say, he probably deserved it.

"You knew she was going to do something bad, didn't you?" Lila asked. "That's why you told me I could leave early if I needed to."

"And why I double-checked to make sure you had your phone," he said.

"It was an experiment, right?" Lila said.

"Which failed miserably," he said.

She leaned back in against the passenger seat, her hand dropping away from the handle. The SUV was getting a bit stuffy, but he didn't start it back up.

"This whole thing," Lila said, "you and me. It's an experiment too, isn't it?"

His cheeks warmed. He had called it that in the beginning. He was beginning to think that was a bad idea.

He was about to say something about that, something that placated her somehow, when she said, "So if this one fails, then what? Do I live with Mom's mom? She says she's not up for raising another kid."

He felt a surge of anger at his Cherise's mother. He didn't need that right now, even though he knew she was right. Her health wasn't the best. He had talked her into seeing his doctor, who was convinced that she wasn't dealing with the death of her daughter as well as she could have been.

"This isn't that kind of experiment," Anton said. The sentence sounded lame. "What I meant when I said that early on was that we'd see how it went with the school and here at the house and, oh, I don't know, the schedule."

She wasn't looking at him. She was staring out of the windshield, her eyes lined with tears.

"You'll be with me always," he said. "We're going to muddle through this together. I'm going to make mistakes, like the one today. But I'm always here for you."

"Until you get smooshed by a car," she said.

The graphicness of her language stopped him. He hadn't expected that. He could say something stupid, but true, like *everyone could die at any minute*, but he didn't think that would be helpful right now.

"I won't get smooshed by a car," he said.

"Mom said she'd be fine whenever she went out, but she wasn't, was she?" Lila said.

"No," he said. "She wasn't."

He wasn't going to blame her either, but Cherise had been driving an older model truck, one that had belonged to her father. She'd been on an errand that required a flatbed—although Anton had never known why.

The truck didn't have the safety features the SUV had.

"But," he said. "I bought this car new when you moved in for a reason. It has all of the newest safety features. We're going to do that every year. People survive accidents better in vehicles like this. And we're going to do as many safe things as we can. That's why we live here."

"Behind a gate," Lila said. She hadn't liked that when they first moved in.

"With security guards who check people coming and going," he said.

"Grandmom says the house is too big. She says no one needs a house that big."

Cherise's mother was the opposite of Cherise, or at least, the Cherise he had met at the All-Star Game. She had been all about the trappings of wealth. Some of that had fallen away as she raised Lila, but not all of it.

"The house is big," Anton said. "Right now, though, we're staying in it."

Lila nodded. Then she said, "That thing with your mom?"

He stiffened, noting that she didn't call his mother her grandmother. Which was good. She was maybe getting it all in perspective.

"Yes?" he said.

Lila turned toward him. "Just don't ever do anything like that again."

"I won't," he said and hoped that was a promise that he could keep.

THE
Santa
SERIES

Nine

Pippa was beginning to like the cheap Santa suits. No one expected her to be anything other than a woman in a costume when she went to the pediatric wings of the hospital with Niko. People smiled at her—if they were up for smiling—and adults winked at her as if everyone was in on the joke.

Everything she was seeing broke her heart, from the sick children to the parents who looked like they hadn't had sleep in years.

She was grateful that Niko hadn't taken her to shelters. He had done a lot of that work on his own, trying to tie his charity to some Nevada charities to see if they could all raise more money together.

Joulu came, too. He had somehow found small items, mostly stuffed toys, to hand out. He had also decorated his suit with some fake fur, glittery gold beads, and a matching belt around his waist.

He had added red-and-green highlights to his wheat-blond hair and painted his nails red, green, and gold. He had offered to do Pippa's, but she kept thinking about what their father would say about tradition and traditional looks, and she declined.

On the Friday afternoon before the run itself, they stopped on the way back to the hotel at an out-of-the-way building near the packet-pickup thrift shop. The building, which was a faded adobe in desperate need of paint, had a sign over the door identifying it as a children's charity. Two old vans with the same sign on their sides were parked outside.

The hatchbacks were open, and four adults, all dressed as clichéd Hollywood elves, were loading boxes inside. Another man, his elf hat sitting on the loading dock railing, was wheeling more boxes to the trucks on some kind of dolly.

That sight looked familiar to Pippa. For all of the magic at the North Pole, sometimes a simple hand truck did the trick better than magical hand-waving and lots of sparkles.

"You don't need to come in," Niko said as he put their van in park. "I just need to check on something."

Pippa already knew what he had to check on. He had been talking with the nonprofit that ran this charity to see if they could figure out how to form an alliance that would benefit both. If they did it right, they would get some government dollars—according to Niko—and certain kinds of tax relief.

He had tried to explain it, but she wasn't that familiar with the Greater World and its arcane monetary rules. She had tuned him out. Joulu had been interested, though, and had asked a lot of questions. She supposed she would talk with Raine later. Raine had a way of explaining things so that Pippa could understand them.

Raine was back at the hotel with her kids. The baby was a little curly-haired blond doll, but his bright blue eyes held a level of mischief that Pippa would see as a warning. Niko and Raine's daughter had Raine's darker coloring, except for the same vivid blue eyes that seemed to be a signature of the North family.

Pippa had enjoyed being with them, but she felt out of her depth with children. She had felt out of her depth on the hospital visits as well, although she had—as Joulu urged her—let her instincts guide her.

The children didn't seem to mind. Many of them had flocked to her, although a lot of them preferred Niko. A number of them asked him, more than once, if he was the real Santa Claus even though he deliberately didn't wear the beard and he was as trim as could be.

They saw something in him that they didn't see in Pippa or Joulu.

Niko got out of the van. Pippa did too, even though she had already told him she had no desire to join him inside. She was just enjoying the mild Las Vegas weather and the sunlight that reflected off all of the white buildings.

She was beginning to realize she preferred the weather here to the weather at the North Pole. She wasn't sure she could tell her family that, though. She knew she didn't want the reaction—which she couldn't quite predict. Either they would argue with her about North Pole snow being essential to all they did, or they would ignore her complaints completely, making her feel even more irrelevant.

It was just a tad chilly—early fall chilly, in her book, not winter chilly—so she kept the Santa coat on. She hadn't been wearing the Santa pants because she learned that they pilled on everything. She wasn't even sure she would wear them to the run.

She didn't lean on the van as she waited for Niko to come back. The van was covered in a layer of dust that it hadn't had two days ago. The dust would get all over the black yoga pants she wore instead of the Santa pants. Even without touching the van, her black boots had gotten dusty. Apparently, Las Vegas was dusty and gritty, even in areas where it didn't seem that way.

The front door to the building opened. Pippa glanced at it, expecting Niko. Instead, the man from the bar— Anton—came out, smiling. He stopped and spoke to one of the fake elves, who laughed and then took the stairs carefully.

Even with his limp, he moved beautifully, another thing that confirmed he was an athlete.

As he headed toward a shiny black SUV, his gaze caught Pippa's. He changed direction and headed toward her. Her breath caught, and her heart rate increased, a reaction she hadn't expected.

"That costume suits you," he said with a bit of surprise. "That looks like it came from the Run On Santa Claus Lane."

"Yeah," she said. "We're heading over there tomorrow, me and my brothers."

She didn't want to explain the real arrangements, which were getting more baroque by the minute, what with Joulu's friends and Niko's family.

Anton looked up and saw Joulu in the van.

Joulu clearly didn't see him. Joulu's head was bent, and he was scrolling on the phone that Tahvo had given him. Tahvo had set them all up with smartphones that didn't suffer as badly in the magic field created by the average S-Elf.

"One of your brothers?" Anton asked.

"Yes," she said.

"He decorated his suit," Anton said.

"He does that," Pippa said and frowned a little. Joulu always embellished his clothes—and they always looked good. Someone should have moved him to fashion or design. There was no reason for him to work with the reindeer.

"And the blond guy who just went in, he's your brother too?" Anton asked.

She nodded, feeling the little ball on the edge of the Santa hat hit her in the back of the neck. She actually felt stupid wearing her family's costume in the winter sunlight of this city.

Or maybe she was just feeling awkward in front of this man. She wanted to impress him and she wasn't sure how.

"Niko's from Chicago," she said. "He's got some business inside."

Anton's eyebrows went up. "I thought I recognized him. Your brother is Niko North, right?"

She nodded, wondering how anyone would recognize Niko. He wasn't a celebrity as the Greater World defined one.

Her surprise must have shown on her face because Anton said, "He's actually a legend in some parts."

"*Niko?*" she asked. Her father was the legend, not Niko.

"What he manages to do as a fundraiser is something most people can't replicate. It's amazing." Anton sounded quite impressed.

Pippa frowned. Niko? Impressing people with his skills at fundraising? It wouldn't have surprised her if he had been good at gift-giving or at finding people something they really wanted, but her understanding of fundraising was that the fundraiser was supposed to force people who didn't want to give anything into giving.

That did not sound like it fit into the realm of S-Elf magic. S-Elves couldn't coerce anyone into giving if they didn't want to. S-Elves couldn't use magic to force anyone into anything.

"You didn't know?" Anton asked.

Pippa let out a sigh. "My family…" She didn't want to say that they were estranged from Niko, because that would maybe disparage him, and she didn't want to do that, not when Anton clearly admired him. "We…don't get to the United States very often."

"You're not American?" Anton asked.

So, in being careful, she had made things worse.

"Well, um, no," she said. "Not per se."

She wasn't supposed to talk about things like nationality. Something like that might upset children from other countries. Besides, the Norths weren't anything, really. The North Pole—*their* North Pole—existed in its own bubble, away from the Greater World. Getting the proper identification to operate in the Greater World used to be a problem, until someone wised up in the middle of the previous century, and set up a bureau for proper identification.

Pippa didn't know if any of that identification was legal or not, but she hadn't cared until right this minute.

"Per se?" Anton asked.

"Well," she said, not wanting to lie to this man for reasons she didn't entirely understand yet, "it's complicated. My family's legal status is really hard to explain."

Anton made a small understanding sound. "That explains your accent."

"I have an accent?" she asked. The S-Elves learned every possible language (and it was easy for them) and were told they were accent-free.

"Oh, everyone has an accent," Anton said. "Yours is vaguely European, but I can't tell from where. You speak with that crisp precision non-native speakers use when they're speaking English."

She frowned, feeling her cheeks heat. She had thought her English was perfect. She had thought *all* of them spoke perfect English.

Anton smiled. He had one of the loveliest smiles she had ever seen. It softened his entire face.

"It's not a crime, you know, to have an accent," he said.

"I know," she said. "I was just told that our use of langu—English was perfect and that no one would be able to tell we weren't from here."

He laughed now. "That's the problem. No native speaker speaks perfect English. Not a one of us. And have you listened to the different ways we talk? I can barely understand anyone from Glasgow or certain parts of the South."

"Oh," she said, unable to say more. Maybe her accent was appropriate to wherever she was. Her father had never said anything about startling English-speaking children in other countries by having a strange accent, and there were no reports worldwide of Santa being American.

So maybe the magic helped S-Elves sound, not like natives, but appropriate enough.

Anton's smile faded. "Did I say something wrong?"

"No," she said. "It's just..."

She shook her head, not sure what to say. How did Niko manage to marry someone from the Greater World? Explaining, even casually, the details of her life was difficult. She couldn't imagine confessing to the biggest secret of all.

"Just?" Anton asked.

She shrugged. "We talked about family the other day," she said. "Mine is a doozy."

"You saw mine," Anton said. "Or, at least, my mother. I would hope you don't suffer with anything like that."

"Not like that," Pippa said. No one in her family would ever hurt a child. "You handled her well. I don't know if I could have stood up to her like that."

And she was fortunate that she didn't have to.

"I never have before," Anton said. "I always danced around her behavior, even when she extorted me for a lot of money. She always came to me when she was broke. But this time, Lila was there, and she was treating Lila like she used to treat me."

His entire body leaned into his sadness.

Pippa didn't know what to say to that. She couldn't say, *You didn't know,* because he probably had and was eternally hopeful. She also couldn't say something stupid like, *Sometimes people change* because she really had no idea if they did or not.

"But you stopped that treatment," she finally said. "You stopped it."

"And I've been apologizing to my daughter ever since," he said. "She's gone through enough this year, what with her mother..."

He sighed and shook his head.

"What happened with her mother?" Then Pippa realized it was none of her business and added, "If you don't mind me asking."

"I don't mind," he said quietly. "Lila's mother died in a car accident a few months ago."

"Oh." Whatever Pippa had been expecting, it hadn't been that. He didn't look like a man who was grieving. But some people managed to keep their emotions private.

He was probably one of them.

"I'm so sorry," she said.

"It's okay," he said, placing his hand over hers. His palm was warm and large, his fingers long and powerful. They sent a tingle through her that she tried to will away.

He's grieving, she reminded herself, for what good that was going to do.

"We weren't married. Lila was..." he shrugged as if he was struggling to find the right word. "...a surprise. At least to me."

It took Pippa a moment to process that. A surprise. In

other words, Lila's mother had gotten pregnant without his knowledge.

"Her mother lived in California," he said. "I would have Lila for the offseason, and—"

"Offseason?" Pippa asked.

"The summer, mostly. I played professional ball for a while."

He didn't even say what kind of ball, apparently assuming she knew. And she had guessed earlier based on his height.

"That meant Lila went to school in LA." He frowned. "I've brought her here, though, because this is also her home. But I'm not sure I made the right choice."

"Being with you has got to be the right choice," Pippa said.

"Being with me is the only choice." He said that a bit fiercely as if that were a battle he'd been fighting.

He squeezed her hand as if he just realized he'd been holding it and then let it go.

This was getting just a little too emotional. Pippa wasn't sure how to negotiate the conversation any longer, so she changed the subject.

She nodded her head at the building. "You work here?"

Anton shook his head. "Coming to local charities is just part of what I do. I teach former NBA players who had to retire early with an injury how to handle their money."

She felt out of her depth with every piece of that sentence. NBA—basketball. She knew that. It confirmed her assumption about the kind of "ball" that he played. But using the words "retiring" and "injuries" in the same sentence didn't really make sense to her.

"The players don't understand charity...?" she asked, not sure if the question was a stupid one.

"Not the way your brother does," Anton said. "They used to see charity as something the association forced them to do, or a line on their tax return or something their fly-by-night financial advisors advised them against."

"Against?" She was really out of her depth now. Why would anyone advise against a charity?

"Yeah. These so-called advisors want the money in their own pockets, not in the pockets of a worthy organization or even the young men themselves." Anton's voice shook as he said this. He was clearly passionate about it. "So many of these young men get cheated because they're dumb about money, and they trust the wrong person."

Then he half smiled at her as if he heard how emotional he sounded. He gave a self-deprecating shrug.

"Rather like I did the other day with my mother," he said, bringing the conversation back where it started. "Thank you for buying my drink."

"It was the least I could do," Pippa said. "I felt so helpless."

Her words hung there for a moment.

"I don't think I've ever been that angry," he said. "It's a heck of a way to meet someone, isn't it?"

She half smiled, not sure what to say. So she stuck out her hand.

"Let's do it again," she said. "I'm Pippa North."

He took her hand and shook it. "Anton Walker," he said and then paused as if he expected some kind of response from her.

Maybe most people did have a specific response. After all, one of the bartenders said they knew who he was.

She couldn't even guess what that response would be. So, she shook his hand one more time for good measure and then let go.

"It's a pleasure to meet you, Mr. Walker," she said.

"Anton," he said.

"And I'm Pippa."

"You'll be at the run tomorrow, Pippa?" he asked.

"Yes," she said. "It'll be our first time."

"Lila's too," he said. "We're just doing the mile."

So were Raine, Niko, and their kids. They had some kind of baby jogger thing that Raine had made Niko buy.

"How about this," Anton said. "How about we meet up at the statue of the peeing boy just before eight—"

"The what?" Pippa asked.

"You'll see," he said. "It's just off Fremont on Third, in front of the D. We can go into the throng together."

She almost said, *I'm sorry, that won't work. I'll be there with my family.* But was she really going to be with them?

Joulu was bringing nearly a dozen friends. They had plans for afterward. She was invited, of course, but she wasn't sure if she wanted to go.

And Raine had already made it clear that she and Niko would finish early and somehow get the kids back to the hotel. *Don't worry, though*, she had said. *Niko will come back for you.*

So it already wasn't the togetherness that Pippa had hoped for.

"The peeing boy," she repeated.

Anton's cheeks looked slightly flushed. "You don't have to. I mean, that's presumptuous of me."

"No, it's not," she said. "I would love to."

He smiled again, that radiant look that she was already beginning to love. "Oh, good," he said. "Lila thought you were nice, and I figured it would be great for her to have a familiar face. None of my friends are going, which surprised me, but we're so nationally oriented that sometimes the local stuff gets lost in the shuffle."

"I understand," she said, and she did. Her family was international, and they seemed to lose track of everything except the Big Day. That's why she had thought it was so revolutionary to come here.

"I am going farther than the mile, though," she said, although she wasn't sure why. Maybe to protect herself in case Anton didn't show.

"I understand," he said with the same solemnity she had just used.

She laughed.

"I'll see you then," he said, and half walked, half ran across the parking lot to a shiny black SUV that clearly hadn't picked up any of the dust she'd been worried about.

"Is that Anton Walker?" Joulu was leaning out the window of the van. "You know Anton Walker?"

Pippa frowned up at him. "You know who Anton Walker is?"

"Played for too short a time before his knee blew spectacularly in a playoff game his team was supposed to win." Joulu was clutching his phone. That made Pippa wonder if he had taken a picture. "I've been following him since he was Rookie of the Year."

"You follow basketball?" she asked.

"Who doesn't?" Joulu asked. "I don't get most of the sports that are popular around here, but that one—it's physical yes, but there isn't all that crashing and crushing and tackling and helmets and padding. No blades on the feet and no unbelievably dull hot afternoons waiting for flyballs in a ballpark."

She didn't understand half of the references, but what she did understand was that she really didn't know her brother at all.

"I can't believe you know him," Joulu said. "Where do you know him from?"

She grinned at him. "I met him at the hotel bar when you ordered me down there."

Joulu laughed which sounded like a series of deep bass bells. The kind of laugh she hadn't heard in weeks, maybe years.

"I *told* you," he said.

"Oh, don't be *that* guy," she said in return.

"Why not?" he said. "*That* guy is both right and a lot of fun."

"What are you laughing about?"

Somehow, Niko had joined them without Pippa noticing.

"Our Pippa just met one of the most eligible bachelors in the entire city," Joulu said. "And charmed him."

"Well, charming is our thing," Niko said. "At least that's what Raine tells me."

"What would a wife know about that?" Joulu said.

"A lot, really." Niko frowned at Joulu. "How do you know about eligible bachelors?"

"I'm more curious how he knows so much about Las Vegas and Greater World sports," Pippa said.

"Greater World anything," Niko said. "I thought I was the only one who lived here."

Joulu banged on the side of the van. Some dust fell off. "I just love being a mystery to all of you," he said and put the window back up.

"I think that might be true," Niko said to Pippa.

She nodded, then looked past him. The SUV was gone.

Eligible bachelor? That made her nervous. She wasn't interested in men who were looking for a relationship.

But it didn't seem like Anton was, not really. He was more concerned about his daughter.

But Pippa had loved the way he placed his hand over hers, the way he had leaned into their conversation.

Maybe she should dial down the North charm. Maybe she should just be a little cooler.

But she didn't want to be. She liked him, and she liked his daughter.

It was just one meeting at...a peeing boy statue.

What could go wrong?

Ten

er first inkling about what might go wrong
was the preponderance of Santas. Once the
van left the confines of the hotel garage,
Pippa began seeing Santas everywhere.

Many of them were getting into rideshare vehicles. Others climbed into limousines, laughing as they did so. Then, as Niko drove them all closer to downtown, there were clusters of Santas, all in the same suit, walking in the same direction.

"This is quite the production," Raine said from the very back. She sat between her daughter's car seat and her son's special carrier, both of which faced backward and were wedged against the seats in front of them—as per law, Niko had said.

Still, Raine sat there, protecting both of them as if the

seats weren't enough. Raine wasn't really an overprotective mom, but she didn't like the way the seats fit into the van—or so she said.

Raine was a tiny woman who had somehow kept her figure after giving birth to two children. She was also a powerhouse. While the Norths charmed people, Raine intimidated them, sometimes with just one look.

Or at least, that was how Pippa had felt the first time she had met Raine at a wedding almost a year ago.

Now, she was getting used to her sister-in-law and really falling for the kids.

Raine was not wearing her Santa hat. She had on the suit, though, with a cute little skirt and some black tights. On her feet, she wore snow boots that made Niko laugh when he noticed them.

When Pippa asked about them, he had said, simply, *Inside joke*, and left it at that.

In the very back was the baby jogger. It was festooned with ribbons and bells and Raine's hat, hanging on a peg where her daughter could reach it if she wanted to.

Raine said it was going to be a balancing act to handle both children for the mile, but Niko wasn't worried.

Sometimes, Pippa thought Niko didn't worry about anything.

Joulu was bouncing in the front passenger seat as if he were the toddler. He had painted his face with a Christmas tree on one cheek and a wreath on the other. Somehow they did not look unbalanced but perfectly festive.

He had dusted his face with glitter powder and glued some fake diamonds around his eyes. He had a tiny candy cane hanging from the right nostril, which Pippa found to be just a bit gross.

Otherwise, he looked more festive than all of them.

"We're going to need a place to meet when this is all over," Niko said, "because we're all going different distances and at different paces."

"How about just at the finish line?" Joulu said. "They'll have refreshments and music and whatnot. We should be able to find each other."

Pippa wasn't sure, but before she could voice her half-hearted opposition, Niko agreed to that.

"I think it would be better if we all went back on our own," Raine said. "From what I'm seeing, this is going to be confusing, and we're not even there yet."

"How?" Pippa said. "I can't carry a phone and do that rideshare thing."

"I think she thinks we should wiggle our noses," Joulu said. "Or whatever. Which might not be a bad idea."

"I didn't know you could do that," Pippa said to Raine. Pippa had thought that Raine's magic was not as vast as the North magic.

"I can't," Raine said, "but I can find Niko. If nothing else, we can meet at the van. We have to bring it back anyway."

Pippa nodded.

"And I'm meeting my friends," Joulu said, then peered at Niko. "You remembered that, right?"

"Yeah," he said, "if I can ever find the Golden Gate parking lot."

They delved into a discussion of closed roads and sideways travel that Pippa couldn't have followed, even if she wanted to. Her heart ached.

This was nothing like she imagined.

Joulu turned in his seat, almost as if he could hear her thoughts. "Why don't you come with me, Pips?" he said. "My friends are *great,* and we're going to have so much fun."

She shook her head. "I—we—were supposed to meet someone, remember?"

"Oh, yeah," Joulu said. "The sexy basketball player."

She felt her face heat. She didn't want to think of Anton as sexy because that made her see him romantically, and she really wasn't ready for anything like that, even if he was interested, which she doubted he was.

"The map says that the Golden Gate isn't far from that pee statue. I'll just bring my friends there. They can't be more overwhelming than five thousand Santas, right?" Joulu smiled at her.

Pippa shook her head again. "He's bringing his daughter."

She wasn't sure how that made a difference, but it did.

"Well," Joulu said. "We can still figure out—"

"No, that's okay," Pippa said. "I'll be all right."

She tried to sound more upbeat than she felt. Joulu studied her. The serious expression on his face made the glitter look faintly like sad clown makeup. Then he smiled.

"This is like going to a super big bar," he said.

She smiled in spite of herself. "It's not, and that didn't work out very well last time anyway."

"Except that you made a tall, sexy friend," Joulu said. "That's how it's done, my girl. One person at a time. And..." he waved a hand at the van, looking around as he did so. "I vote that we make our own way back. You can do that, right, Pips? I'm never sure what magic works for whom."

"If nothing else, I'll walk," she said, inclining her head toward the window. "That seems to be the choice du jour anyway."

And it did. The closer they got to Fremont Street, the more Santas they saw. Santas clustering near a parking meter. Santas waving their hands at each other as if arguing about directions. Santas walking in and out of various casinos as if this were a Santa convention.

Niko turned away from the preponderance of Santas and headed toward a part of the city that Pippa hadn't seen. There was a railroad bridge and some construction in the distance. Then he turned right on Main Street and found even more Santas walking quickly.

He passed them and carefully turned the van into a parking lot. There were no spots, but he didn't seem to care.

"There! There! There they are!" Joulu said, pointing at a white limo draped in red crepe paper.

Pippa squinted at it. Eight people stood around the limo, watching the street. They were all wearing Santa costumes, but every single one was customized. Two women wore headbands with elf ears on springs. A person of indeterminate gender had covered every part of their costume in gold glitter. They seemed to be trailing it everywhere.

Niko parked behind the limo, and Joulu turned.

"Come with me," he said to Pippa. "You'll love my friends, and they won't mind if you run off with the basketball player."

"He's bringing his daughter," she said again.

"As if that matters," Joulu said. "She'll like everyone too. Come on."

Maybe Pippa would have been tempted if she hadn't met Anton. Or maybe not. She felt out of place around those exuberant people.

"Maybe next year," she said.

"Oooo," Joulu said as he pushed open the door. "She's discussing next year already."

He waved his fingers and launched himself out of the van. Exclamations of *Hey, grrrl,* and *Who is that delicious man with you?* and *Joulu!* rose around them all.

The van door closed, and Niko drove forward, avoiding even more Santas.

"Do you know where to park?" Raine asked.

"I do," he said. "I reserved us a spot."

He drove down what looked like a side street and entered a large parking garage. He had to stop to take a ticket, and then drove inside.

There were cars parked everywhere. Niko followed a string of cars up a concrete ramp and around in circles until he reached level five. There more cars were parked or parking. A handful had their trunks open. People were putting on their Santa beards or pulling on their coats and laughing as they did so.

Their joy was infectious. Pippa smiled despite her disappointment.

Maybe her father should see this to understand the impact of his image. Or maybe the Old Men in Charge should.

But then they'd just take credit for it as if it were all their idea.

In some ways, it had been. Their marketing got the ball rolling, but it had slipped away from them a very, very, very long time ago.

Niko parked, and Pippa slid out, putting her hands behind her back and stretching. She was ready for the run, even if she was going to do it alone.

She was trying not to let the disappointment eat at her. This was not at all what she imagined. As usual, she was alone in a sea of runners, someone they weren't going to notice, someone who could literally disappear midway through the run, and no one would realize it at all.

The disappointment must have shown on her face because Raine came up beside her, the baby tucked under her chin.

"Walk with us, Pippa," Raine said. "It'll still be fun."

Pippa was tempted. But she wanted to run. She'd been looking forward to that. Besides, Raine and Niko were—in some ways—a closed loop. When they looked at each other, Pippa felt like she didn't exist at all.

Pippa made herself put on a brave face.

"I think it'll be fun no matter what," she said and smiled. "I'll meet you all back at the hotel."

"You sure?" That was from Niko. He clutched the baby jogger in both hands.

From inside the van, a little voice wailed, "*Daaaaaaaaaadeeeeeeeee!*"

Niko smiled and put the jogger down. "Coming, punkin," he said, then he raised his eyebrows at Pippa. "Raine's right. Come with us."

She shook her head. "We can compare notes when we get back," she said, and headed for the stairs before someone tried to talk her out of this again.

The stairs were concrete and filled with Santas, chattering and in a hurry, adjusting their hats, their beards, their suits. Most of the conversation was about the upcoming show, which apparently was held on Fremont Street. Celebrities and local TV anchors gave instructions and sang and kept the crowd under control until the race got underway.

Pippa followed a Santa that was twice her size and was holding the hands of two little kids. They were picking their way down. The Santa—a man—was answering their breathless questions.

She didn't mind following because their joy was infectious.

They reached ground level, stepping onto a sidewalk. They paused—and so did she, trying to figure out where this mysterious statue was.

She had looked it up before leaving, so she knew the cross streets. She just had to find them.

The nearest one went directly through the crowd of Santas, crossed Fremont Street, and then to the street where the statue was. She was going to have to shove her way through the throng.

Or, at least, that was what she thought. Instead, there was a slight opening that the crowd left for people like her —Santas like her, since everyone in front of her, behind her, and beside her was dressed exactly the same.

As she made her way past one of the biggest Christmas trees she'd ever seen across the covered area that defined Fremont this far west, she began to worry that she never would find Anton and Lila. Joulu had been right; she should have gone with him. Or maybe with Niko and Raine.

Now, Pippa was going to have to decide how long she would wait for Anton because she didn't want to miss the start of the race. It was some time off—the crowd would cue her as to when to move to the starting area on Las Vegas Boulevard—but still.

No one else was going to be there with her. Anton wasn't going to show up either. That was just the way things worked for her.

That was the way they had always worked and the way they would work now.

Eleven

Anton regretted choosing the peeing boy statue as the meeting place. He hadn't been thinking like a father; he had been thinking of the best place to locate someone in a sea of Santas.

He stood next to the statue, which was slightly blocked off. It was of a young boy peeing into a fountain. Apparently, it was based on one in Brussels.

Unfortunately, it was amazingly lifelike—in all ways. On this day, the boy had on a Santa hat, but usually, he didn't wear anything. And he was always violating the fountain.

Lila was fascinated. She was peering up at it, examining the boy's bits as if she hadn't seen anything like them.

And maybe she hadn't. She didn't have siblings or

cousins, and she was too young to babysit. He doubted she had seen anything in childcare either or at school.

"This is cool, Dad," she said. Sadly, she was referring to the fountain and not the Santas. The Santas had left her alarmed. There were too many of them, and she wasn't doing well with crowds right now.

He had listened to Kwame. Anton made sure the Santa costumes he and Lila wore were distinctive enough to see from far away. They were both wearing gold scarves around their neck, tied in the French way, so they looked just a little fashionable. They were going to be hot, though, because the temperatures were already in the high fifties.

Lila's hand was toying with the edge of her scarf already.

Anton didn't say anything, though. He wasn't planning on letting her out of his sight, so even if she took it off, he would be able to find her.

Behind them, on Fremont Street, a band started playing "Santa Claus Is Coming to Town." The squeals of a public address system being set up rose over the sound of the band.

Some of the nearby Santas turned and headed onto Fremont.

He shifted from foot to foot. He really didn't know Pippa North, so he had no idea if she was the kind of woman who made plans and then never showed up.

He hoped not. He had enjoyed their conversations, as awkward as the first one had been.

But, if she was anything like her brother Niko, she'd be reliable. And probably good-hearted.

Although Anton already knew she was good-hearted. The way she had helped Lila with just a look and a glance when his mother was making a scene in the atrium bar had told him that.

A hand lightly touched his elbow.

He looked down. Pippa North stood beside him. Her Santa hat was pushed backward, revealing her ivory skin and bright blue eyes. Her blond hair curled around the edges as if the hat had been made specially for her.

She was wearing the jacket, which fit her perfectly and showed off her slender form, but instead of the pants, she wore black leggings. The boots she had worn the day before were gone, replaced by what looked like a brand-new pair of off-brand running shoes.

"Thanks for waiting for me," she said, sounding a little out of breath.

There was something in her tone, a relief, maybe. Perhaps she had thought he wouldn't be there.

"My pleasure," he said. He looked around her but didn't see any more tall blonds. "Where's—?"

"My family didn't come," she said and looked away. Still, he could hear the disappointment in her voice.

He understood it. Being raised by a mother like his, with his father mostly out of the picture, made moments like this one all too familiar. Anton was determined not to be a parent like that for Lila.

Lila stopped looking at the statue as if she was going to be tested on its details and made her way to the two of them. She held out her hand in perfect politeness, just like Cherise had taught her.

"I'm Lila," she said.

"Pippa." Pippa smiled. "It's nice to be formally introduced."

"Yeah." Lila let go of her hand and fiddled with the scarf again. "My dad says you work with this charity."

Pippa frowned at him, not understanding the question. Anton shook his head ever so slightly. Clearly, someone had misunderstood.

"Um, actually, no," Pippa said. "My brother runs a big charity in Chicago so he's here for inspiration. I...um... have a different job."

"Oh," Lila said in a tone that made it clear that adult stuff bored her. "Where'd you get your costume?"

"Same place you did," Pippa said.

"Yours is prettier," Lila said.

Pippa shrugged. "They probably used different vendors."

But she really didn't sound convincing. To Anton's unpracticed eye, the costume had the same lines and edges, but Lila was right: there was something different about the way that Pippa wore it.

"You gonna walk with us?" Lila asked.

"I was hoping to run this," Pippa said, "but my brother asked the same thing. I'm beginning to wonder if I should walk."

"No," Anton said. "Do what makes you happy. That's what this race is about."

"Your brother is here?" Lila asked, looking around. "Where?"

"Actually," Pippa said, "both of my brothers are here, but Niko is with his wife and kids, and Joulu is with some friends."

"Joulu?" Lila said. "What kind of name is that?"

"It's a pretty standard old Norwegian name," Pippa said.

"Is that your accent?" Lila asked. "Norwegian?"

"No," Pippa said, and Anton could see the irritation on her face. The accent thing all over again. He had no idea why it bothered her so much. "It's hard to explain where I'm from."

Anton was even more curious than he had been earlier, but he didn't want to interrupt this conversation. He hadn't seen his daughter engage with an adult that she wasn't required to engage with since she moved here. And she didn't seem to notice that Pippa was white, which he thought of as a step forward.

"It's weird," Lila said, "that his name sounds like 'yule' and it's nearly Christmas."

Pippa smiled. "He was born in December."

"So it's not a coincidence," Anton said.

"Not even close." Pippa's smile held secrets. He would love to tease them out of her.

Behind them, though, the PA had fired up and someone was shouting into it. He hated when an inexperienced person used a PA and thought they needed to shout to be heard.

"Should we see what that is?" Pippa asked.

"No," Lila answered that really fast. "There's too many people in there."

She hadn't liked crowds from the beginning, probably because when she was little, Anton had been at the peak of his fame, and she had been poked and prodded and pushed whenever she was near him.

"There's a lot of performers," Anton said. "We could hang back if you want."

Lila shook her head. "This is okay."

"There will be a lot of people in the race," Pippa said gently.

"We'll be moving," Lila said as if that made all the difference. Maybe it did to her.

Moving. Anton heard that. "Well, then," he said. "Let's head to the starting line."

"Can we?" Pippa asked. "Do the organizers mind?"

"I don't think they'll mind," he said. "I don't think they expect to control five thousand Santas."

Pippa laughed, and it sounded like bells—a thousand bells jingling beautifully up and down the scale.

Anton realized he had never heard her laugh before, nor had he ever heard anything quite so entrancing.

Lila looked at her as well, as if she couldn't believe what she had heard.

"Santas are extremely difficult to control," Pippa said, and it almost sounded like she had some kind of private joke in mind.

Anton wanted to ask her about it but wasn't sure if it would be appropriate around Lila. She still believed in Santa, and he didn't want to do anything to get in the way of that.

They walked down Carson, the street parallel to Fremont, along with a handful of other Santas. Then Anton had them walk to Fremont because he wasn't sure exactly where the start line was. He hadn't ever walked to it on his own. He had been led past it.

Dozens of Santas took pictures of the sea of red and white behind them. Others posed with casino doors, bar openings, and the supersized menorah that dominated the center of the closed-off street near Fourth.

Lila gawked at everything. Anton kept pace with Pippa, who seemed to be taking it all in as well.

"I never realized..." she said, her voice trailing off.

"What?" he asked.

She looked at him as if weighing what to tell him. He'd seen that look a lot, once on the face of a surgeon who told him that he would never run again—not like he had. Anton had tried to prove that surgeon wrong and had made everything worse.

"My family's work..." she started, then shook her head. "The family business, it's about Christmas."

"Really?" Lila asked, and Anton felt irritated at his daughter for butting in. He had to swallow that emotion. It wasn't fair to her. "How is that possible?"

"Lots of businesses focus on the holidays," Anton said.

"I was asking Pippa," Lila said.

"We...um...we—it's a narrow brand," Pippa said after a moment. Anton realized just how carefully she was choosing her words.

"What's that?" Lila asked.

"It's an old business with one singular focus," Pippa said, "and I hadn't realized just how..." She shook her head. "I can't explain it."

She looked to Anton. He smiled at her.

"Business can be hard to explain sometimes," he said to her, but really, he was talking to Lila.

Not that she was listening. Pippa had done it right; using words like "brand" and "focus" she had bored Lila and sent her skipping toward a stand filled with Run On Santa Claus Lane merchandise.

Anton followed her over. She was touching everything from the Santa necklaces to the Santa T-shirts. Fortunately, none of them had rude sayings and all of them had the name of the charity on the back.

Pippa stopped beside them as well. She was frowning, not an angry frown. More like a thinking frown.

"Care to share?" he asked.

She looked up at him, her blue eyes so clear he could get lost in them.

"It's really complicated," she said. "Business stuff."

"I'd love to hear more sometime," he said.

She smiled, but her face closed down. She looked back down at the merchandise, poking at a Santa backpack complete with beard.

"Can I get some, Dad?" Lila asked.

"Do you want to carry it for our walk?" he asked.

She pursed her lips as if she was weighing the option. But instead of saying no, she said, "Get something on the way back?"

Anton's gaze met the gaze of the woman behind the table. "Will you be here long?" he asked. He knew some of these spots on Fremont were rented by the hour rather than the day.

"Until noon," she said.

"Thank you." He turned back to his daughter. "Then the answer is yes."

She jumped and did a few half cheerleader half karate poses, the first joy he'd seen from her in a very, very long time.

"Yes!" she said, and skipped down the street a little.

"Well, you made her day," Pippa said.

"Finally," he said, blinking hard. His eyes were wet,

but he wasn't going to call those tears. "Shall we continue?"

"Sure." Pippa rapped her knuckles on the edge of the table as if she were trying to put something in her head. Then she led the way to Lila, looking back once—not at Anton, but at the sea of Santas behind them.

He waited until she turned before wiping at his eyes. Little steps, the therapist had said. Lila would take little steps.

But it seemed to him that she had taken a big one today.

Twelve

T he Old Men in Charge had no idea what they had unleashed on the world, Pippa thought as she turned the corner onto Las Vegas Boulevard. It had been shut down for the next few hours so that people could complete the run. The Boulevard stretched ahead of them, and there were Santas everywhere. Apparently, the full five thousand hadn't been crammed into the Fremont Street Experience after all.

Lila stopped when she saw the sea of Santas ahead. The smile left her face. She looked back at Anton, alarm making her eyes seem brighter than they had before.

"We don't have to go," he said to her.

"Sure we do," Pippa said, reaching out her hand. She was going to use some Santa magic to calm this girl. She was much too panicked at much too young an age.

Lila looked at Pippa's hand. "I don't really want to anymore."

"Oh, I get that," Pippa said, keeping her hand out. Then she crouched. "My family, it has the weirdest expectations of people. And everyone but me and Joulu work really hard during the holidays, so we can't celebrate together."

"Really?" Lila was breathless. Anton watched her intently. "Don't you miss them?"

Pippa felt there was more to the question than Lila actually expressed, so she didn't want to give a flip answer.

"They have to work," she said. "We have family time after the holidays."

"My Daddy was like that," Lila said. "He had to work at weird times when he was playing basketball. Now he's more normal."

Anton smiled, his lips tight as if he was trying not to laugh.

Pippa tried to ignore him, but it was hard. She was very aware of his nearness. Lila still hadn't taken her hand. Pippa wanted her to, but wasn't going to will her to do so using any of her own magic.

Lila looked at the sea of Santas. More were joining all the time. Far ahead of them was a gigantic arch with a Santa head on top. That had to be the start line.

Photographers stood on the stairs of a nearby parking garage, and a few stood on the roof. People who were not in Santa clothes and who apparently hadn't gotten the memo stared at the growing crowd of Santas in awe.

"So you understand about schedules," Pippa said.

Lila nodded. That was good because Pippa knew she was taking the long way to get to her point.

"Because of their schedules," Pippa said, "I have to do a lot of holiday things by myself. I started doing runs all over the Grea—"

She stopped herself briefly, astonished she was so comfortable with this child and her father. Pippa had almost blown it. She had almost said "The Greater World," and that would have raised a lot of questions.

"The world, really," Pippa said. "I've gone all over the world, and it was weird. Because every country is different, every run is different, and at first, I was just like you."

Lila frowned. Was that the wrong thing to say? Pippa couldn't tell.

"How?" Lila asked.

"I had never seen so many people. I—"

"Oh, I've seen them," Lila said. "They don't like me. They want my dad."

She had clearly gotten caught in something to do with celebrity and it had scarred her. Anton closed his eyes for a half second as if the very idea upset him.

But Pippa couldn't pay attention to him, not right now. She needed to focus on Lila.

"This crowd is not here for your dad," Pippa said gently.

"They came once for him," Lila said. "He was the grand marshal."

"Lila," Anton said, "that's—"

"There's a different grand marshal this year," Pippa said, "and I don't think anyone even knows who it is."

"They don't?" Lila asked.

"Do you?" Pippa asked.

Lila looked at her dad, who shrugged. "Noooo."

"They're here for the season. They're here to celebrate. And they're here to have fun." Pippa heard herself. She hadn't associated the holiday season with fun, maybe ever. Her family didn't either.

Lila looked at the crowd. It had grown even bigger since they started talking. Some Santas were walking around them, and no one was even looking at them. Most of the Santas were laughing.

A big brown dog on a leash sniffed Lila. She looked down and smiled. The dog wore a Santa hat and a red tutu.

"Marly," a woman said, tugging on the leash. The dog didn't move. It was probably because of Pippa. Animals liked S-Elves a little too much.

The woman came over and grabbed the dog's red and green collar. "I'm sorry. She usually doesn't act like that."

"She's cute," Lila said. "Can I pet her?"

"Sure," the woman said.

Lila patted the dog's head with the flat of her hand. Obviously, she had never been around dogs before.

"Like this," Pippa said and petted the dog's head, then scratched under her chin. The dog tilted her head back and sat down, tail wagging.

Lila imitated her. Pippa was about to touch her, to send some warmth, when Lila stopped.

"Thank you," she said to the woman very formally.

"You're welcome," the woman said and led Marly away.

"You stopped," Pippa said.

"She wanted to go," Lila said. "She kept looking at all the people."

She being the woman, clearly, not the dog, who had been watching them.

Pippa was a bit startled at how sensitive Lila was. "That was kind of you."

Lila nodded, then looked over her shoulder at the crowd.

"You said you were like me," Lila said, her voice soft. "You didn't like crowds?"

"For a completely different reason," Pippa said. "I'd never seen so many..." Wow, she almost said *mortals*. She really was relaxed around this child—and her father. "...people in one place. It's unnerving."

"Yeah," Lila said softly. "So what did you do?"

The moment of truth. Pippa couldn't lie to her. "Well, I figured I was already there, so I might as well try."

Lila squinched up her face. She didn't seem to like

that. But Pippa wasn't going to change what she had to say just because Lila didn't want to hear it.

"But I promised myself I could leave at any point," Pippa said. "If it was too overwhelming or scary, I told myself I could just walk away. No harm, no foul."

Lila smiled. "My dad says that."

Anton didn't add anything to that, though. He was standing still, listening.

"Did you ever leave?" Lila asked.

"Once," Pippa said. "In Russia. There was this winter garden…"

How could she describe any of that? Russia had become a cold and terrifying place. It had always been difficult, but it had gotten a lot worse.

"…and I just didn't like it," Pippa said. "So I didn't stay very long."

"But you went," Lila said.

"I went," Pippa said.

Lila sighed. Then she looked up at her dad. "Can we leave?"

He looked disappointed. Pippa was disappointed, too.

"I suppose so," he said. "Did you want to go back to the merchandise table?"

"Not *now*, Daddy," Lila said. "If I want to. Later."

"Oh." He sounded as surprised as Pippa felt. "Um, sure. Yes. Of course."

He glanced at Pippa, eyebrows up, his expression much lighter than it had been a moment before.

"Okay, then," Lila said, taking her dad's hand. "Let's give this a try."

They plunged into the crowd, Lila leading, Pippa trailing slightly behind as if she had Lila's back. Anton's heart was pounding. He couldn't remember ever being this nervous—not for something like this.

Going to get Lila after Cherise had died, bringing her home, trying to be the best dad, yeah, those things had made him nervous, but not this heart-pounding anxiety that left him feeling like something could go very wrong.

His daughter led him into the crowd. There were Santas everywhere. Some were adults talking to each other. Some had on sashes with the names of law firms or something personal. A black sash caught his eye. It said *Bride*.

He thought that a little weird.

There were dogs of all sizes, some in wagons. Children in strollers and people with baby joggers. No one stood too close to anyone else, unlike at sporting events or even some of the speeches he had given way back when. And people here parted for anyone coming through.

Lila tugged him forward, going deep into the crowd, which surprised him.

It wasn't until they had gotten half a block in that he saw where she was heading. She was going toward Marly, the dog.

The woman who owned the dog was standing with a couple of other women. They were of different races, some as Black as Lila's mom and others as pale as Pippa. A handful appeared to be mixed race. He realized at that moment that Marly's owner was too.

He felt a moment of satisfaction, not just at Lila's behavior but at the city that enabled it. He had been worried about some of her outbursts, but something had changed for her. Maybe just being around all different kinds of people.

Pippa was keeping up. She smiled when she saw the woman who owned Marly.

"Mind if we pet her again?" Pippa asked.

Anton hadn't thought to do that. Simple politeness, which he usually harped on, and he had been the one who hadn't done it at all.

"I think she'd love that," Marly's owner said.

And then there were introductions all around, most

of them too fast for Anton to keep up with, but Pippa was participating. Lila was crouched, petting the very calm dog and maybe even talking to her.

She didn't let go of Anton's hand, though. Close, but not too close.

He smiled at Pippa, who smiled back.

After a few minutes, Lila stood and said to Pippa, "You're going to walk with us, right?"

"Pippa was planning to run," Anton said. "We should let her."

Lila put on her brave face, one he had seen too often of late. She nodded.

"I'll walk with you," Pippa said. "It would be my honor."

Fourteen

nd it was. She felt like she belonged with Anton and Lila, not like she was intruding as she had with Niko and Raine. The women and Marly were going to walk too, and they became a unit, a rather protective one, once they realized that Lila was still very nervous.

Pippa hadn't had to use her magic at all, which was probably for the best. She had been taught from the beginning not to alter people's emotions if she could at all prevent it.

Her father only used that skill if he had to when he stumbled on someone who felt threatened by him during that long holiday night.

It took quite a while for the race to start. The grand

marshal and the people in charge walked to the race with even more Santas behind them. The grand marshal—who was too far away to be seen clearly—and some of the others came to a big stage the back way.

A woman talked too loudly into the PA system, and then the crowd started counting down from ten. When they reached one, the crowd moved as a unit. It didn't run forward. It surged, though, as if everyone was ready to go.

It took a few moments for the surge to reach their little group. As they got to the start line, a man dressed like a gigantic reindeer pointed the two directions—5K in one lane and one mile in another.

Pippa looked at the 5K runners, weaving and dipping through Santas that were stretched ten wide across one side of the boulevard. She could veer off and run the 5K, and no one would be upset at her.

Or maybe Lila would be, but Lila was a good kid. She wouldn't say anything.

Pippa thought about it and almost veered, but as she did so, her heart sank. She wanted to walk with Anton and Lila. She followed the one-mile signs with her newfound friends, who were laughing and pointing at various modifications to Santa costumes, not to mention the occasional green Grinch.

Pippa had to go slower than she had thought. Everyone was strolling, not power walking. She had to reassess. She usually thought of movement as exercise, not enjoyment, but almost everyone around her was enjoying it.

Even Anton, who, by this point, was limping rather badly.

"You okay, Daddy?" Lila asked, looking concerned.

"I'm great," he said, and he sounded that way. Not fake-great the way people did sometimes when they were putting on a brave face, but as if he was really enjoying himself.

Pippa could probably put a hand on his knee and take the pain for now. But she didn't suggest it. She was just beginning to get to know Anton and Lila, and she didn't want to scare them with what they could consider to be healing powers.

So she slowed even more. That let her see the crowd and the makeshift signs everywhere. Big posters were on the Boulevard, all declaring Santa Claus Lane open for business. Little signs underneath pointed the way. The red ones were for the 5K people, and the green ones showed the mile.

Music blared from the first one-mile turnoff on Clark, heading down past some government buildings toward Sixth. Someone was blaring "Here Comes Santa Claus" on a music system. She doubted that person was sanctioned by the organizing committee, but she could be wrong.

Her group, led by the dog Marly, turned left while the

runners continued forward. Pippa watched them go—realizing that was her last chance to join the 5K.

Anton must have seen the look on her face.

"Go," he said. "You came to run this. Go enjoy yourself."

Actually, she had come to unite her siblings, and she had failed at that. That thought had been making her sad for days, but the sadness was gone now. She almost felt like she had found a new family, but she doubted that happened this quickly, particularly when she didn't even know the names of some of these women.

Lila slipped her hand into Pippa's. That sent a jolt of surprise through Pippa. She had tried to get Lila to take her hand before, to make Lila feel better using magic, and instead, Lila used no magic at all to make Pippa feel better.

"I am enjoying myself," she said to Anton.

He smiled. She had fallen in love with that smile. She had a hunch she could fall for the man, too.

She had no idea what that would do to her future, her family, or her life.

"This is weirdly fun, isn't it?" he asked.

They had reached Carson Street, a little over a block from where they started. The walk would end very soon. She could actually see the finish in the Llama Lot.

The Llama Lot, which was the name of the parking area where the festival had set up. Pippa had no idea why it was called the Llama Lot. She just figured it was more Las

Vegas weirdness. This part of Santa Claus Lane had signs decorated with pictures of Santa, arm around a llama instead of a reindeer.

Lila was the one who pointed that out.

Pippa smiled, thinking of her father. He rarely hugged anyone, let alone some tall, weird-looking animal.

Again, some music blared ahead, only this time, it was the Chuck Berry version of "Run, Run, Rudolph," and, as far as she could tell, it was being played by the organizers themselves.

"You look thoughtful," Anton said, then looked down. He clearly noted his daughter's hand in Pippa's, and it didn't seem to bother him.

"I'm just amazed at how much people make Santa their own," she said.

"Santa and the holiday," Anton said. "Everyone finds a way to make it special for themselves."

Lila let go of Pippa's hand and skipped forward, apparently her fear of the crowd gone. Marly kept up with her, not running, but more as if it were the dog's responsibility to keep an eye on her.

That gold scarf helped, even though the crowd had spread out. Most of the walkers were behind them despite the slow pace that Anton needed.

"I hadn't realized," Pippa said. So much of the holiday was curated from the North Pole. "Santa Claus Is Coming to Town" was written with the encouragement of the Old Men in Charge. They had provided the "inspiration" for the lyrics, which might've meant that they sent the lyricist a dream.

It might've meant that they were working with him too. Pippa never really kept track of the history of marketing because she kinda sorta thought of it as a history of manipulation.

Maybe it wasn't. Maybe it had been something else.

"I thought your family had a holiday business," Anton said.

"It does," Pippa said. "I do the scheduling for all the departments for the entire year."

Which sounded like less work than it was.

"If I don't have it done and ready by your Thanksgiving, then I have screwed up."

"*My* Thanksgiving?" he asked.

He was catching her in all kinds of revelations. Maybe she wanted him to.

"Yeah, well, you already heard my accent," she said. She heard herself; she sounded a bit grumpy about it.

"So you're not working right now," he said.

"Well, in theory, we—" she almost did it again. She almost said, "S-Elves" "—um...are working all the time."

"That doesn't sound like fun."

He was right; it wasn't. She hadn't realized it. No wonder she ran. She had to work off the stress somehow.

Curiously, though, she was feeling none right now.

Instead, she was feeling inspired. She had a hunch no one at the North Pole understood these runs or their counterparts, the Santa Pub Crawls. The people at the Pole saw them as marketing opportunities—although they studiously stayed out of any charity events, making sure that the charities got the best opportunities to fundraise on their own.

No one at the North Pole understood how much the image of Santa had grown beyond them. They complained about movies like *Bad Santa,* and they didn't like some of the portrayals in the media, but they thought those were aberrations.

They didn't see these events and the positive images of Santa as something that they could use to expand their reach, maybe even do some of the things Niko was trying to get them to do, like take care of the children who had gotten missed.

Her family—and the North Pole itself—had to move into the Greater World more. They used to do that about a hundred years ago. Now, though, they didn't, preferring to be hands-off.

That was a mistake.

"Something has you intrigued," Anton said, and she looked at him in surprise. No one had ever correctly identified her moods before.

"This is so inspiring," she said as she watched Lila stop skipping and rough up Marly's ears. "I can see some changes at home because of this."

Anton's smile tightened. "When are you heading home?"

He actually sounded...interested? Concerned? She couldn't believe that he would be concerned, but maybe he was. Maybe there was something here between them.

Only she wasn't sure she could believe in it. So, she focused on what she could believe.

"I don't have to head home yet," she said. "I don't really need to be back until the planning sessions mid-January."

"Not even for the holiday?" he asked quietly.

"Ironically," she said, "we don't have time to celebrate it."

"I meant the one you mentioned afterward."

"Oh, that." She never thought of it as a holiday. It was more like a vacation with a party because their father —and all the other elves—did not want to repeat anything about Christmas itself. "I can skip it if need be."

And she had, occasionally, to do some first-of-the-year runs. Her favorite had been in Zurich—an actual marathon that started at midnight of the new year. She had felt inspired that year as if she could do anything.

It had been a long time since she felt like that.

"Why would you?" Anton asked.

"It's more of a bacchanal than a holiday celebration," she said, astonished at herself. The words slipped out of her mouth unexpectedly, yet again.

They had turned onto the last three blocks on Fremont. The music had gotten even louder—some Santa

Claus song that she didn't recognize but Lila clearly did. Lila was dancing.

"Look at her," Anton said with pride in his voice. "She hasn't smiled like that since September."

"I'm so glad this worked for you," Pippa said. "And I'm glad I could see it."

He put a hand on her shoulder, not as if he were trying to control her or even hold her down, but maybe as a silent question about whether or not she wanted him to touch her.

"I'm glad you could too." He smiled down at and she smiled at him, and it felt like A Moment. She hadn't ever shared a smile like that, which made her feel so alive.

They reached the turn onto Tenth, which funneled them toward the finish line. Lila ran back to them, Marly trailing. The women had been near the dog the entire time, and they were still laughing, discussing all that they had seen.

Lila slipped between Pippa and Anton and held both of their hands. "Let's cross together," she said, and so they did.

A photographer stood right at the finish, taking everyone's picture. Some high school students gave out medals with a grinning Santa on one side and one of the designs for Santa Claus Lane on the back. Pippa was just glad the design did not show a llama.

She put it around her neck.

"Hey!" Lila said. "Santa!" Which seemed like a strange

thing to say, considering there were hundreds of Santas already in this parking lot. Some were shopping at the merchandise booths. Others were donating to the charity. Still, others were buying hamburgers at a barbecue stand that was sending fragrant smoke into the air.

It took Pippa a moment to see what Lila meant, and then Pippa's heart sank yet again.

That wasn't *a* Santa. That was *the* Santa, her dad, sitting on a red and green and gold throne, surrounded by children. It was almost as if he glowed. His suit looked pristine and a bit old-fashioned, with its fur collar and cuffs. His boots reflected the sunlight, and his white hair was thick and flowing.

But his beard was what set him apart. It was fluffy and white but somehow didn't stick out the way that the beards on fake Santas did.

Even from here, though, she could see his bright blue eyes. They sparkled with such force that they seemed to draw people in.

She felt a surge of anger. He was checking up on her. He had encouraged all his children to participate, and they had not. They hadn't even walked together.

She wished she had a place to go hide. But she knew better. The Real Santa (and she always felt like she needed a little trademark attached to his name after thinking that) would be able to find her if he wanted to.

It was one of his many gifts.

So, she hung back.

Lila ran forward and got into the already long line of kids, all of them chattering happily.

Of course, they were. They were about to have the most authentic Santa experience that little kids had had since Pippa's great-grandfather had decided to visit Macy's Department Store one year.

"What's wrong?" Anton asked.

She supposed she could tell him half of it. One part would make no difference at all.

"That's my father," she said.

"That...?" Anton frowned, so she nodded at the stupid, glowing, perfect Santa on a throne in the middle of a parking lot. "I thought your family wasn't going to be here."

"They weren't." She remained rooted, watching the joy the kids were displaying. Some of it was the magic in the air that floated up from the most authentic S-Elf in the world. But most of it was real, the sheer leftover exuberance of the run mixed with what promised to be a great Santa experience.

She watched her father work. She hadn't seen it for a long time. He placated crying children who were smiling by the end. He laughed long and hard, the magic of his deep-throated "ho-ho-ho" making others laugh heartily around him. He nodded and promised and somehow managed to move the line along as if he controlled time itself—which he did, mostly around himself, particularly on Christmas Eve.

"I have to say," Anton spoke quietly, "that is the best Santa I've ever seen."

"It had better be," Pippa said.

He looked at her sharply, but she didn't explain. She didn't know how. What was she going to say, anyway? *Of course, he's good. That's the Real Santa.*

She would sound like a nut.

"Oh, good God. Is that Daddy Dearest?" Joulu had reached her side. His merry band of friends were heading toward the food and the other entertainment, although all of them stopped briefly and looked at the Real Santa because how could you not?

"Yeah," Pippa said.

Joulu shook his head, and then looked away as if he had seen a car accident and didn't want to examine the blood any longer.

"I hate watching him work," Joulu said. "It always makes me feel so inadequate."

Pippa understood. She knew she could never do any of the work her father did, not as well and not with such concentration. She was about to say so when Joulu turned away from their father.

Instead, Joulu focused on Anton. Joulu looked Anton up and down and then said, "And...*you* are the sexy NBA star that my sister met in the atrium bar...on my suggestion."

Pippa's cheeks heated, but Anton laughed. "*Former* NBA star," he said. "I could barely walk that mile."

"Oh, well, if you're good, Pippa will fix that for you," Joulu said.

"What?" Anton asked.

"Haven't you told him, darling?" Joulu asked. Then, with a merry twinkle in his bright blue eyes—reminiscent of their father, although Pippa would never tell Joulu that—he wandered off, muttering something about the race providing hot cocoa or else.

"Told me what?" Anton asked. "I thought you worked in scheduling, not physical therapy."

"I do work in scheduling," Pippa said. "Sometimes my brother is a world unto himself."

"Are we discussing Joulu?" Niko had reached them. He was dragging the baby jogger behind him with one hand. Both children were asleep, which was probably a good thing because it prevented him from having to explain the presence of their grandfather in full Santa mode.

"It's better than discussing Dad," Pippa said, waving a hand at their father.

Raine was behind the baby jogger, and she stepped to one side, peering at him. "Wow," she said. "I've never seen him in action."

"The best Santa ever, am I right?" Anton asked.

"Actually," Niko said in all seriousness, "I hear our great-grandfather was better."

Anton grinned and extended a hand. "Anton Walker," he said. "Big fan."

"Of Santa?" Niko asked.

"Of you, dummy," Pippa said. "He's heard of you."

"I've actually watched you work," Anton said. "The way you can fundraise—I've never seen anything like it."

Niko flushed bright red. "I—um..." he looked at Pippa for help, but she wasn't about to bail him out of this. "I...charm is a family trait. So I try to put it to good use."

"And you do," Anton said. "Rather like your father over there."

"Oh, my father has his own special magic," Niko said, with just a hint of resentment.

"Do you know what he's doing here?" Pippa asked.

"I thought you did," Niko said. "You're in charge of the schedule."

"This was not on it, for him, anyway."

The line of children was thinning. Most of the families had done the mile. A handful more children were trickling in, but Santa's literal moment in the sun would fade soon.

Pippa sighed. Rather than cower next to her brother, she probably should face the music, whatever that meant.

So she walked toward her father. He acknowledged her with a twinkle and then returned to the child standing near him on the platform surrounding the throne.

Pippa realized at that moment the child was not sitting on his lap. She was leaning toward him, though, hand on his arm.

It was Lila. And for some reason, Pippa felt like that was a budding disaster.

Pippa was close enough now that she could hear the conversations near her father. She focused, as she had learned to do in S-Elf training, and heard only Lila's voice—and Pippa's father's, of course.

"You're not telling me your greatest want," her father said.

Lila looked sad. "My daddy says it's impossible."

Pippa's father waited patiently. Pippa realized he was giving Lila all the time in the world—literally. They were in a tiny bubble that he had somehow extended to Pippa, maybe so she could hear—and everyone else was moving very slowly outside of it.

"You can tell me," Pippa's father said with great compassion.

Lila's eyes filled with tears. "I want my mom back," she said.

Pippa's breath caught. She had never really listened to her father deal with real children before. And real children had real needs, as Niko often said.

"My daddy says you can't do that," Lila said, almost apologetically.

"Your daddy is right," Pippa's father said very softly. "I wish I could bring your mom to you, but I have no power over life and death."

"Then this is all made up, isn't it?" Lila asked. "Stupid stuff about presents and I-wants and nothing real, right?"

Pippa's father sighed. He put out his hand, and Lila took it.

"Your mom loved you," he said.

Lila nodded, her mouth turned down.

"She loved you enough to last you your entire life," he said. "That love is still here. You just have to remember it and figure out how to touch it, every single day."

Lila stared at him, one tear trailing down her cheek.

Pippa waited for her to explode in anger, but Lila seemed to be thinking about what Pippa's father had just said.

"She wouldn't want me to be unhappy, then, right?" Lila said, voice unsteady. Obviously, someone had told her that, maybe more than once.

Pippa's father smiled. It wasn't a full Santa smile. It was a warm, personal smile meant only for Lila.

"I think she would want you to feel your emotions," he said. "Grieving is what we do when we lose someone. It's up, and it's down, and wanting them with us—that's normal."

"That's what my daddy says." Lila wiped at her face with her free hand.

"He's a wise man," Pippa's father said. "You're lucky to have him."

"But not forever, right?" Lila said, clearly parroting what someone else had said to her.

"Nothing is forever, Lila," Pippa's father said.

"You are," Lila said.

Pippa's father shook his head. "Two hundred years ago, my family took over the North Pole. Before that…"

He let his voice trail off because, as Pippa knew, the story of before wasn't really for children.

Lila didn't seem curious about it, though.

"So I'll never see my mom again?" Lila asked.

Pippa's father put on his most serious face. "That's not for me to say. In this world, though, no. You will not."

"I don't like this world, then," Lila said.

Pippa's father tilted his head as if he could see inside her. "It has your father," he said. "Your mom's mother. Your cousins and some new friends."

And with that, his gaze met Pippa's. She started. She hadn't expected him to know about that, but then, he was her father and the Real Santa. He knew way too much about way too many things.

"You might want to add a dog to that," Pippa's father said.

"Marly?" Lila asked.

"Marly has a person. But I bet Marly's person will help you find a dog like Marly."

"Can you bring me one?" Lila asked plaintively.

Pippa's father looked directly at her again. Pippa sighed. She'd been part of this kind of subterfuge before. Technically, S-Elves weren't supposed to traffic in living beings, but sometimes they managed to pull it off.

"If your father approves," Pippa's father said.

And so, of course, Pippa couldn't say no to that. He

had given her an out if she wanted to take it, but she nodded anyway. She would help.

"I'd *love* that," Lila said, wiping at her eyes again. Then she leaned forward and hugged Pippa's father. "Thank you, Santa."

"You're most welcome, child," he said, and somehow, with that, he managed to let her know their conversation was over.

Lila didn't seem to mind. She scurried down the platform and out of the bubble.

Pippa remained.

"That wasn't fair," she said. "You didn't give me the right to refuse."

"Oh, but I did, child," her father said.

"What are you doing here?" she asked.

"I told you all that I wanted you here. Three of you listened." He smiled. "I'm glad of that."

"Why?" Pippa asked.

"Because my job is about more than running a compound and traveling too many miles on the longest night ever invented," her father said. "It's also about understanding the Greater World."

She leaned back just a little.

"You three, you like the Greater World, don't you?" he asked.

"I—can't answer for the others," she said, even though she knew the answer. They liked the Greater World enough to spend a lot of time in it, just like she did.

"But you do," he said.

"Yes," she whispered.

He smiled at her. His fatherly smile, not the one he shared with the world. "Now," he said, "I must get back to work."

He waved fingers at her, and it felt like she was pushed out of the bubble. Children stepped up on the platform and climbed on his lap. The line had grown a bit, but not as much as she would have thought from all of that time.

It still unnerved her how he could manipulate time like that, and she'd been around it all her life.

Pippa staggered back to the group she had just left. Niko and Anton were deep in conversation, gesturing as they talked. Raine was soothing the baby, and Lila was standing at the edge of the line, staring at Pippa's father.

Then Lila saw Pippa and smiled, joining her as they walked back to the group. The women were still talking with each other, and Marly had fallen asleep at their feet.

Lila stopped to pet the dog. As she did, she leaned in, whispering something in Marly's ear.

"You all right?" Niko asked as Pippa joined them.

"Yeah," she said.

"You talk to him?" Niko asked.

"A little," she said.

"Is he mad?" he asked.

"Not at us," she said.

Lila finally joined them. Marly and the women were on their way out of the parking area. Pippa watched them leave. They were passing the line of children, which really wasn't a line any longer. Just two or three kids waiting for their chance to talk to Santa.

"You talked to Santa," Anton said to Lila, and it seemed to Pippa that he was nervous. He had known what she would ask.

"Yeah," Lila said.

"Care to tell me what you asked for?" At least Anton knew the protocol. Let the kid think the request was private.

Lila sighed, and Anton tensed. Pippa waited, too. Niko was watching them, clearly unsure what was going on.

"You don't mind a dog, right, Dad?" Lila asked.

"A dog?" Anton looked surprised. He had clearly expected something else. "I've never had a dog. How do we get a dog?"

"Santa takes care of it," Pippa said with a little force.

"Nonsense," Niko said, and Raine butted in.

"What he means," she said, rocking the baby, who was still half asleep and clinging to her red suit, "is that you'll have to take care of any animal who shows up at Christmas."

Then she glared at Niko.

"Right," Niko said. He frowned at Pippa because he knew the living beings rule.

It's okay, Pippa mouthed.

He nodded, then shrugged.

"A dog, huh?" Anton said. He looked a little panicked.

Pippa wanted to reassure him but wasn't sure how. So she remained quiet.

She looked over at her father. He was talking to the last child, and that conversation seemed to take a while. He was probably letting the bubble slowly burst.

Lila was watching as well. Intently, in fact. Anton looked over just as the child—a little boy—ran to his mother with joy on his face.

Then Pippa's dad stood. He climbed off the throne, put a finger alongside his nose, and rose up into the air before vanishing.

"Did you see that?" Lila asked.

"See what?" Anton asked. The effect was the same as it always was. Children could see the magic of an S-Elf. Adults could not. "Where'd that Santa go?"

Fortunately, he hadn't told Lila that the Santa was Pippa's father.

"He disappeared, Dad," Lila said. "He put his finger alongside his nose and nodded, then—"

"'Up the chimney he rose,'" Niko said, trying to cover.

Lila glared at him. "Yeah. He rose into the air, and then he went away."

"I didn't see that," Anton said. "But I don't see him either."

"Because he *disappeared*, Dad," Lila said.

"There's still a lot of Santas here," Pippa said. "He's probably lost in a group of them."

"He's *not*," Lila said. "He *vanished*."

"Santa magic," Raine said, glaring at her husband.

"Yeah," Lila said.

"We need to respect it," Raine said.

Pippa was liking her more and more. "We do," she said.

"Whatever that means," Anton said.

Lila walked over to the throne as if she was going to inspect it. Niko started to follow, but Raine grabbed his arm.

"Let her," Raine said. "She'll figure it out."

"That's what I'm afraid of," Niko said.

"She's eight," Pippa said. "That's okay."

"What does that mean?" Anton asked.

Pippa had done it again. She had spoken freely around him.

"She needs to believe in magic as long as possible," Raine said.

Anton looked at all three of them. "There's something you're not telling me."

"That's right," Pippa said and quickly changed the subject. "I'm going to help you get that dog if you want. Your decision."

Anton frowned. "I've never had a dog." Then he shrugged. "But I've never raised an eight-year-old before either." He looked at Pippa. "You're okay with helping?"

"It's my pleasure," she said. And it was. It meant that

she'd be around Anton and Lila more. She liked them. She liked them a lot.

"She can't unwrap it on Christmas morning," Anton said.

"We'll worry about logistics later," Pippa said. "It shouldn't be hard, though. I can deliver the dog you've chosen that morning. Or we can give her a rain check for an animal shelter so she can pick out the puppy herself."

"Puppy," Anton said, sounding shell-shocked. "That means potty training."

"Yep." Raine laughed. "You'll be fine."

"I hope so," he said, then looked at Pippa. "*Thank* you."

She nodded.

He walked over toward Lila, who was still staring at the throne.

"You like him," Raine said.

"Yeah," Pippa said.

"A lot," Raine said.

"Yeah." Pippa wasn't looking at her. She was still staring at Anton and Lila as they talked about the throne. She could imagine the discussion. Lila was probably telling him about her experience.

"He's a good man," Niko said. "Good heart."

"Yeah," Pippa said.

"You two have a future," Raine said.

Pippa finally looked at her. "Oh, I don't know. That's a big word."

"It is," Raine said. "But I can see it."

"Trust her," Niko said. "She has some amazing abilities of her own."

Pippa let out a breath. "I don't know...."

"You're going to have to tell him about our family," Niko said.

"Slowly," Raine said. "He's the kind of man who is going to have to hear about it slowly."

"Hear about what?" Anton had returned with Lila.

"Puppy care," Niko said, lying for Pippa so she didn't have to. "If there's a dog involved, there will be puppy care."

"If there's a dog in our future," Anton said, looking down at Lila, "I'm not the only one doing puppy care."

Lila laughed. It was a great sound. "Okay, Dad. I get it."

Anton stopped beside Pippa. "Are you sure about helping? This is your time off."

She smiled at him. She liked being with him. And *like* was probably too small a word.

"I'm okay if you are," she said. "I'd love to help, even after the dog moves in."

He smiled at her. She was right: *like* was too small a word. She loved that smile, and she really...well, she didn't want to say *loved* because it was too early...but she really cared about the man behind that smile.

"Can I ask you a weird question?" she asked.

"Sure," he said.

She straightened, feeling nervous for the very first time. "How are you with magic?"

"You mean like stage magic? I don't like it much," he said. "It's fake."

"I mean real magic," she said.

"As in magical moments?" he asked.

"Sure," she said, not wanting to reveal much more. Niko and Raine were watching intently. Lila was still staring at the throne, lost in her own thoughts.

"I'm…I wasn't…a believer," he said. "But I think there are things that are hard to explain. Like the way a dog brightened my daughter's day so thoroughly, she forgot she was afraid of crowds."

"Real-life magic," Pippa said. Not the kind of magic she was referring to, but it would do, at least right now.

"Real-life magic," Anton repeated, confirming what she said. "I suspect my daughter is going to make me see things a whole new way."

Daughters do that.

The words echoed around them. Anton looked up. Niko closed his eyes in annoyance. Pippa felt a shiver run down her back.

Her father was watching. Damn that song. Sometimes, he really was everywhere.

And she wasn't exactly sure what he meant. She would have to ask him.

Later, when she left this strange little Santa Claus Lane in the middle of Las Vegas.

"Do you hear that?" Anton asked. "About daughters?"

"Hear what?" Raine asked, all innocence.

"That daughters...oh, never mind," Anton said. "Anyone up for lunch? I'll buy."

"I'd love that, Daddy." Lila had turned her attention back to them.

"Sure, why not," Niko said, looking at Pippa as if he expected her to object.

"Should we find Joulu first?" Pippa asked.

"He's with his friends," Raine said. "He'll be fine."

"Pippa?" Anton asked a little too intently. "Lunch?"

"Yes," she said.

He smiled at her again. Then Lila said, "Hey, where's that throne?"

Pippa looked over. There was a bit of magical glitter where the throne had been, but the whole thing was gone.

Damn the elves. They should have waited until the entire crowd had dispersed.

"I didn't see anyone move it," Anton said. He sounded a little agitated, and she didn't blame him. In the Greater World, it would probably have taken a few guys and a truck to remove a throne of that size from the parking area. "How did that move?"

He looked at Pippa, and she realized that since he knew that Santa was her father, she would know how the throne moved.

She looked pointedly at Lila, who was listening.

"I think," Pippa said slowly, letting Anton know with her eyes that this was also for Lila's benefit, "we should chalk this one up to magic, don't you?"

"Um..." he looked a little distressed. Then he glanced at his daughter, who was smiling. Her smile was so similar to his that it melted Pippa's heart. "Yeah. Magic."

Lila clapped her hands together, startling the baby. While she was apologizing to Raine, Anton leaned closer to Pippa.

"Promise me you'll tell me how all of this worked later," he said.

Pippa's heart rose ever so slightly. That was something she could do.

"I promise I'll tell you everything," she said, and she would. She would tell him, and she knew, somehow, through that undercurrent of magic all S-Elves lived with, that he might resist at first, but eventually, he would understand.

She slipped her hand in his. He squeezed it tightly.

They leaned into each other. Raine saw it and glanced at Niko, who grinned.

"Sometimes," he said, "the Big Guy knows more than he's letting on."

Pippa frowned at him. She didn't like to think that her father knew that she would meet someone like Anton. But her father had known that Pippa was connected to Lila.

S-Elf magic.

She was going to have to teach Anton all about it.

She found that she was looking forward to it.

She was looking forward to the entire season—for the first time in forever. She had been right to come here after all. She hadn't assembled the family she had been born into, but she had discovered people she wanted to spend her holidays with.

And that was, perhaps, the best gift of all.

Up On The Rooftop

JULKA STOOD ON the roof, hands on her hips, feet covered in snow. She was tired, she was cold, and she hadn't felt the tip of her nose in hours. She was staring at yet another fancy-pants chimney, a narrow little pipe sticking up out of a lovely square pile of fake bricks, and she wanted to kick it.

Which wasn't very festive of her.

But seriously, who felt festive on October 30th? It was New England, for heavens sake. There wasn't supposed to be snow for another—oh, what? Two weeks? She really didn't know, except that she had checked the records going back to the 19th century, and never found a snowfall as deep as this one *before* Halloween. She wasn't supposed to be this cold for another month, and by then, she should've been moving south. Where she would have to deal with freezing fog, sleet, and sheets of ice.

Oh, joy. Ho-ho-ho and all that.

It was her own damn fault that she was standing here. She was the one who had said, *I don't have the skills to run a workshop, but I can find problems and solve them.*

And then, of course, she had to go too far, because she always went too far: *Besides, I don't want to stay here for my entire life. I'd like to travel. I need to see the world. I really, really do.*

She sighed. When she had said she wanted to see the world, she had hoped she would be placed in one of the many year-round outposts. She would receive toy shipments, interview local children, and make certain that the back-up sleighs were in fantastic shape. She would scout local products and find great toy factories that didn't even know they would be enlisted.

She had wanted to be one of the Ambassadors for Santa's massive worldwide operation.

She hadn't meant that she wanted to be a minion in Entry Access Quality Control, someone who had to view each and every house with children in it for the appropriate entrance. Appropriate, in Santa's rather medieval mind, always meant a chimney.

She sighed and clutched the tablet to her chest. It was a real paper tablet—one of the millions of Big Chief tablets that someone in Santa's North Pole headquarters had stocked up on in the 1960s, along with stubby Number 2 pencils that she refused to use.

She wanted an electronic tablet—a gizmo, with bells and whistles and access to the worldwide web (even though, she'd been told, no one called it that any more). The workshop had hundreds of those as well, but not for the elves or the human support staff, but for the tech-savvy children who didn't want a dolly or a train set, but who wanted the latest in computer gadgetry.

Everyone at the North Pole had to be careful with gadgetry. Many types of magic—particularly fairy tale magic—weren't compatible with electronics. Elven magic also had difficulty with electronics. Santa always had the Fairy Kingdoms design his systems, and that didn't always work well.

Delbert popped his head out of the invisible sleigh. She hated the effect. It made him look like he'd been beheaded, and she had gotten stuck with the head part. She wondered what the civilians on the ground saw. Whatever it was, it couldn't've been pretty.

Entry Access Quality Control wasn't supposed to call attention to itself. That was why the invisible sleigh, which was the same size and shape as Santa's (only without the reindeer; they hadn't needed reindeer since 1930 or so, but they kept the reindeer for form's sake. Besides, the reindeer had a hell of a union).

Delbert usually remained invisible as well. He was an S-Elf, sharing a lineage with Santa. Delbert hated his heritage, and would've fled long ago except that he couldn't hide who he was, no matter how much he wanted to. All those photos of Santa vacationing on the beach, of Santa in Hawaii in the summer or lounging in Monte Carlo instead of driving his sleigh—well, they weren't Santa.

They were usually Delbert.

And as punishment for tarnishing the Santa brand, he had to spend one year on Entry Access Quality Control.

"Well," Delbert said, "do I have to put my boots on?"

"No," Julka said sourly. He might have been punished by doing Entry Access Quality Control, but she was the one who suffered. She inspected, kicked, shook, and fought with more chimneys than she wanted to consider. Yes, she had the best boots and gloves that magic could conjure, but she still got cold and wet and *grumpy*.

Delbert only had to emerge when there was a likely chimney, which there hadn't been all day.

The rules of Entry Access Quality Control were pretty simple: if the chimney didn't work, and the skylight looked too dicey, then Santa got to use any available door. And Delbert didn't have to check the doors. With the growing obesity problem worldwide, the entire slew of Santa Advance Teams no longer had to worry about doorways being too narrow for the Jolly Old Elf.

"I'll boil up some lunch then," Delbert said. "You gonna want any?"

"No, thanks." She couldn't stomach a second day of

Peppermint Veal Stew, even if the elves did think it a delicacy. Her stomach didn't. Neither did her taste buds. That was the other problem of traveling with elves. They preferred sweet foods to almost everything else, turning the most disgusting things into candy.

She'd grown up with it, but that didn't mean she liked it. After the last few days, she deserved something made here in the Greater World, not that it was greater than the North Pole's magical universe. The Greater World was just bigger—and lacked the magic.

Which she was really beginning to appreciate.

Because magic—what little of it she had—was making her cold.

MARSHALL COLLIER SHADED his eyes with his right hand, and looked up at the roof. It wasn't a trick of the light. He was seeing a slight figure holding some kind of notebook kick a chimney. Tiny runnels of snow trickled down the side of the rooftop, like the precursors of an avalanche.

Or at least, a severe loss of roof-snow that would ruin the shoveling work he had managed earlier this morning.

Marshall had a narrow flatbed truck that could hold a small Caterpillar tractor with a large shovel on the end, and two different size snow blowers. He also had real honest-to-God shovels tucked into the back and three changes of clothing, including pairs of boots.

He'd been out clearing side streets and sidewalks since 5 a.m, calling the power company every two blocks or so to report downed lines, and doing his best to be a Good Samaritan.

This freak pre-Halloween blizzard, and his parka, had given him a kind of anonymity that he hadn't had since the Great Recession began. It hadn't mattered that he hadn't worked for the fraudulent companies that caused the meltdown. What mattered was that he had made a lot of money (too much money) as an investment banker and venture capitalist. It also didn't matter that he had retired from that business in 2007 at the age of 34. What seemed to matter to all these folks who were struggling to pay their now-overpriced mortgages on their meager unemployment benefits, was that he had once worked in that industry, and that meant he was one step above Satan.

And maybe he was. When he worked in the industry, he hadn't thought that there were actual people behind the numbers. He wasn't a sales guy. He had been an analysis guy. He hadn't dealt with people; he had dealt with numbers.

As the economy tumbled into darker and darker places, he had watched the news reports with horror, realizing that each number he had played with had represented someone else's money.

The thing was, he hadn't been told that when he was hired straight out of Harvard. No one said a word as he had manipulated the numbers, stroked and fondled them and made them grow—legitimately—until the returns he got weren't good enough for his bosses. They wanted him to cheat on the math. He never cheated on anything. Not on tests, not on girlfriends, and certainly not on something as important as his job.

So he got fired for not taking enough risks. But he had already taken a big risk: he had put some of his earnings into a buddy's company. The company looked dicey from the beginning, but a friend was a friend, right? He had then invested in a few other companies, calling himself a venture capitalist, when really he was a depressed fired former investment banker.

And then his buddy's company became a huge success. And Marshall, as one of the early investors, made a fortune.

He pulled out of the venture capital business because he didn't want to make his fortune into an obscene fortune, especially not while his neighbors were starving. So he concentrated his efforts on helping charities become more efficient—manipulating numbers again, but for a good cause. (And giving away money.)

But he never talked about any of that, and everyone in this rather toney neighborhood thought of him as that investment banker guy. Hated, as if he had robbed all those funds all by himself.

He had no idea why he kept trying to ingratiate himself with the people in this place, but he did. He kept telling himself it was because he liked his house and he didn't want to move—which was true—but honestly, it might've been because he was trying to ingratiate himself with himself. He had let himself become part of the problem, and he really hadn't tried to implement a solution, back when there could have been one.

Guilt. It went a long way. Including getting him out at 5 a.m. on a blizzardy morning, clearing roads and driveways for people who would spit on him if they knew he was the one behind the wheel of the snow blower.

Still, six hours of work later, he was feeling pretty good. He wasn't cold, he wasn't wet, and he had managed to clear miles of roadway and driveway by his own rather mighty self.

Sometimes good physical labor felt a lot better than massaging numbers. Even if that meant he was seeing the same people over and over again on rooftops.

Although that wasn't really accurate. He was seeing the same *person* over and over again on rooftops. She was tiny, slender, and stylish, wearing a little red cape with fur trim. (He hoped it was fake fur trim. In this neighborhood, wearing fur could get her killed.) She also had on reddish pants tucked into knee-high boots. She was wearing fur earmuffs and no gloves at all. And she looked cold.

When he had first seen her, he thought she was a child. She was so slim and so regal, and her outfit so outlandish for someone going from roof to roof, that he figured she had to be about twelve. A few houses ago, he had gotten closer, and realized if she was twelve, she should've been locked inside the house.

She had a curvy figure appropriate to her small size, and golden blond hair that he hadn't seen outside of shampoo commercials. He couldn't quite see her face, but her body language wasn't twelve either. It was exasperated adult—or it had been, until she gave the chimney in front of her one frustrated kick.

He frowned at her. He had no idea why a woman dressed like she was heading for a Macy's Christmas photo shoot would travel from rooftop to rooftop in a MacMansion-filled Connecticut neighborhood. Nor did he know exactly how she was doing it. Or what angered her about it so much.

He did know that he found her fascinating, from the tip of her golden hair to her impractical boots. He wondered if he should yell up at her and warn her that too many sudden movements would cause the snow to slide off the roof—and her with it.

Then she stomped away from him, toward the back of the house. She reached the peak of the roof, stepped up some kind of ladder that he couldn't see—and vanished.

And not a wink-out disappear complete with little sparklies. Nor was it like a transporter vanish in *Star Trek* where the entire body fuzzed into a multicolored light show. It was as if she got swallowed by something. First her head and shoulders disappeared, along with one of her feet and an arm, then her torso, and finally the remaining foot. All that remained was a disturbance in the Force (as Obi-Wan would have said), which looked rather like a heat mirage, floating briefly next to that chimney.

Then nothing. Nothing at all. Not even the house next door. At least, not for a few seconds, anyway. It was as if someone had set up an opaque wall, designed to match the snow and the gray cloud cover (which was threatening even more ugliness).

He blinked and the neighbor's rooftop reappeared. And so did a few more rooftops he hadn't known were missing.

Okay, that was it. Six hours of physical labor in the cold, moving tractors and snow blowers and piles of snow, subsisting on stale (lukewarm) coffee, breakfast bars, and one apple, had not done him any good.

It was time to take a break. It was past time to take a break.

He sighed, rubbed his eyes, and headed to lunch.

IT HAD TAKEN Julka fifteen minutes to convince Delbert that she needed to stop at the Burger King two miles away. He just wanted to go to the next rooftop. He had some vision of getting done before night-fall. Like that was going to happen. They wouldn't be done until the morning of December 23rd. Although to be fair, he was only referring to this town, and in this town they only had 35 houses left to go.

Besides, they had already earned hotel money. Julka liked that best of all. The teams that couldn't get their quotas done in the time allotted had to sleep in their sleighs. But Julka and Delbert were one day ahead of schedule, partly because of the blizzard. They'd worked around it, using the North Pole Navigator to let them know when and where the worst of the weather would be. Then they would go to the safest part of their region, get the work done, and move onto another area, avoiding most of the snow the entire time.

The Burger King's roof had been shoveled off. It had a single pipe that spewed smoke that smelled of frying beef. A gigantic Halloween pumpkin balloon had been shredded by the blizzard's middle-of-the-night winds and hung off the roof like orange streamers. Since reddish orange was one of Burger King's primary colors, the streamers looked planned.

Nothing else did. The parking lot was jammed. Julka had to convince Delbert to land on the nearby health club's roof. She had hoped to land in the parking lot.

But the parking lot—which was huge—was also full.

She sat on the roof's edge, feet crossed, watching as locals streamed into that Burger King. Rules dictated that she wait until no one was around, so that she wouldn't be seen, which was one reason why she chose the health club's roof. But if she waited much longer, she'd eat shingles.

A guy with a huge rig filled with all kinds of snow-moving equipment parked in the auxiliary parking lot, as far from anyone as he could get. He climbed out of his four-by-four, pushed the hood of a parka off his head, and wiped his face.

He had beautiful black hair in need of a trim. He was

tall and broad-shouldered, and moved with the ease of an athlete. He didn't look up as he walked, and she felt oddly disappointed. She wanted to see his face.

She had a feeling she'd seen him before, but she had no idea where.

She lost sight of him in the scrum of vehicles in the main parking lot. He had been the last non-magical person in her line of vision. She grinned, then launched herself off the roof.

Jumping from rooftops had not been one of her magical skills until she took this job. Then she got an augmentation just so she was protected from accidental slippage or falls of more than three feet. This was the best perk of all—that feeling of floating through a cushion of air. It made her feel like she could fly if she would only put her mind to it.

She landed on the sidewalk outside the health club. She adjusted her hair and her ear muffs, hoping she looked enough like a regular person—a regular American person —to get by.

This was the one thing she had little experience with, the one thing she valued the most: the opportunity to mingle with regular people, the kind the Pole was designed to help. She knew she could never quite blend in, but she could at least experience everything like the tourist she was, making memories, snatching moments out of other people's every day lives and wondering what she would have been like if she had been born in New England instead of the North Pole.

She squared her shoulders, adjusted her cape, and headed for the front door.

THE
Santa
SERIES

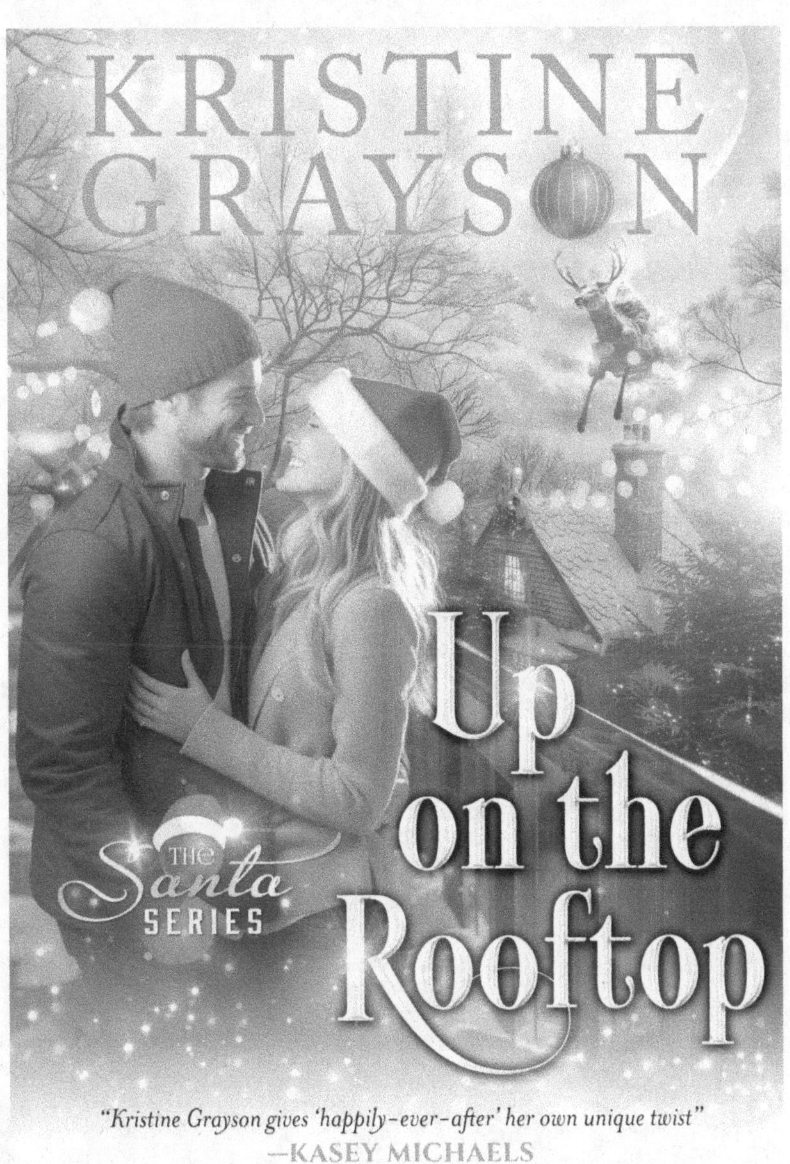

Keep Reading *Up On The Rooftop!*
Go to *WMGbooks.com*

But Wait, There's More!

Want more holiday goodies?

Go to wmgholidayspectacular.com.

Hear Directly From Kris!

Keep up with the latest news, releases and so much more
—even the occasional giveaway!

To sign up for the Kristine Grayson newsletter, a pen
name of Kristine Kathryn Rusch, **go to kriswrites.com.**

You can also **follow Kris on Bookbub.**

About the Author

Called "The Reigning Queen of Paranormal Romance" by Best Reviews, bestselling author Kristine Grayson (also known by her real name, Kristine Kathryn Rusch) has made a name for herself publishing light, slightly off-skew romance novels about Greek Gods, fairy tale characters, and the modern world.

Her novel Utterly Charming, won the Romantic Times Reviewer's Choice Award for Best Contemporary Paranormal Romance.

She writes in several series, including the Fates Series, the Charming Series, and the Santa Series.

Her Daughters of Zeus Trilogy is YA set in the same skewed universe, and she writes Middle Grade stories about the daughters of Cinderella and Prince Charming.

As Kristine Grayson, she also edits the romance volumes of Fiction River: An Original Anthology Magazine.

For more information about her work, go to kriswrites.com and sign up for the Kristine Grayson newsletter.

facebook.com/kristinekathrynruschwriter
patreon.com/kristinekathrynrusch
bookbub.com/authors/kristine-kathryn-rusch

www.ingramcontent.com/pod-product-compliance
Lightning Source LLC
Chambersburg PA
CBHW010735100726
47899CB00009B/3054